COURTING LIGHT

A. ZUKOWSKI

Part of
SEASONS OF LOVE
Anthology

Beaten Track
www.beatentrackpublishing.com

Courting Light

First published 2018 by Beaten Track Publishing
Copyright © 2018 A. Zukowski

All rights reserved.

ISBN: 978 1 78645 256 6

Cover Design: A. Zukowski

Beaten Track Publishing,
Burscough. Lancashire.
www.beatentrackpublishing.com

ACKNOWLEDGEMENTS

To the boy who likes to draw lights.

Hey, Jason, you remember Hebden Bridge and the fly that committed suicide by diving into your drink?

Ellie, sing me the song in your perfect pitch. Pretty please.

Thank you, A.M. Leibowitz and Andrea Harding, for your careful beta-reading.

Sometimes we have stories that we need to tell but are afraid to. Perhaps they are too personal, or they are simply too emotionally demanding to write. So, we put them aside, forgotten like dreams in the morning. When I saw the call for this anthology, I remembered one of those stories. I was reluctant, both because I knew it'd be a difficult one to write and because I write slow. Writing to deadline isn't my forte. Somehow I found it in me to get my arse in gear to complete this novella. Thank you, Debbie McGowan, for your wonderfulness, and for including this story in the collection. I look forward to reading all the other diverse stories.

In the short time since I 'joined' Beaten Track, writing has become a less lonely pursuit. Thank you for your encouragement, my fellow Beaten Trackers.

CONTENTS

Courting Light 1

Day 1 3

Day 2 15

Day 3 25

Day 4 35

Day 5 39

Day 6 45

Day 7 49

Day 8 55

Day 9 61

Day 10 71

Day 11 75

Day 12 79

Day 13 83

Day 14 89

About Seasons of Love 95

About A. Zukowski 96

By A. Zukowski 97

Beaten Track Publishing 98

COURTING LIGHT

I T WAS THE summer before I started college. I was eighteen and didn't feel particularly clever even though I was on my way to become a university student in September.

DAY 1

"A RE YOU ONE of the volunteers? Get your arse in here," a young woman bellowed, her voice bold and impatient. I couldn't see her face since she stayed in the front cab of the van. When I caught her profile in the side mirror, a pair of Jackie-O sunglasses obscured her face. "Come on, jump in and shut the door behind you."

I learned later that 'come on' was a favourite phrase of hers.

I did as I was told and climbed onto the back of the transit van, struggling to slide the heavy metal door behind me. It shut with a loud clang. I turned to face the dozen or so people who were already seated. Searching around for an empty space, I could see that my fellow volunteers were mostly young and in their twenties. I'd probably be one of the youngest since they only allowed over-eighteens as helpers.

They were mostly women but I found two guys among us. Clad in T-shirts, casual jeans and trainers, the dozen or so faces were fresh and eager. I felt apprehensive and cursed myself for thinking this working holiday was a great idea. One of the guys stood up and let me climb over the crowded bench to sit by the window. He smiled. I noticed the freckles on his face and the rosy cheeks, as if he hadn't quite grown out of his baby fat.

I stared out, then, and saw about twenty adults of varying ages and sizes waving to the other van that was idling a few parking spaces down. Some of the kids' faces pressed against the glass. I knew they were under eighteen, but they seemed to represent a wide range from about six to big kids, teenagers who were in fact not much younger than me.

What was I doing? The guilt surfaced alongside nerves. Did I qualify as a carer only because they had some kind of disability? Was it purely selfish to do something I was clearly untrained for just to gain some experience? For my benefit? For my curriculum vitae?

Several of their parents linked hands, as if their offspring were being taken to meet their fate with the Gestapo, not a summer camp. Worry lines spread across their foreheads. I saw a woman in her thirties dab her eyes with a handkerchief, trying to wipe away her tears. That did nothing to ease my nerves. *What if I accidentally hurt* her *child?* The responsibility weighed me down. I wished they had rejected my application.

I turned back to survey my fellow helpers instead. I wondered if they were seasoned carers who knew what they were doing. Fear was probably obvious on my face. My seat mate nodded as if hearing my inner voice.

"My name's Tim." He held his hand out and I shook it. "They're worried about their kids. That's all."

"Josie." I should have offered further information but my brain froze. My reticence didn't seem to bother him. He carried on with the serendipitous induction. I obviously looked like I needed it.

"You're doing them a big favour. Believe me. It's not easy being a carer twenty-four seven. For some of the parents, these two weeks once a year are a life-saver."

"Some of them don't look very happy." I thought of the crying mother.

"They never get a break looking after their children, but they're also terrified of leaving them in our hands for two weeks. Some of the kids are quite severely disabled. You'll see," Tim explained patiently.

No shit. I would *not* want to leave a child in my hands.

My mum had a good job as a hairdresser. She'd been working in the same salon for twenty years. We didn't have money problems, but I never had the kind of relationship with her like other daughters seemed to have with their mothers. I didn't care about my hair, make-up or looking pretty while those things were her livelihood. Mum was emotionally distant, especially so after my parents divorced when I was ten. She had boyfriends, dudes who came and went, but she never remarried. I had a hunch that she resented having two kids—I also had a know-it-all older brother—as we made her less eligible in the dating market, but she didn't have much of a choice. That was why she'd left me mostly to my own devices. Dad was absent. He took up with another woman. We knew where to find him if we needed to, but that was about it.

After the holidays, I was going to study sociology at a university in London. I had the vague idea that I wanted to know about 'society'. Having read a few key texts during my A' Levels, I had impulsively put it down as my first choice for a degree. I would leave my home town and start a new life. For that was how I'd imagined being at university—behaving like an adult, living independently and making new friends.

So, I gathered that it was my first summer as an adult, and I needed to get out there, to be part of *the* society. I wanted to volunteer for the summer camp because I'd lived such a sheltered life that I didn't believe I was remotely qualified to study the subject. Of course, much later on, I realised that sociology was as removed from the way we lived as it could be. I would spend hours arguing about structure and agency, and theorising capital and labour. Then, I decided that I'd like to see how care workers dealt with kids. I thought I'd be helpful and contribute something for once. Besides, the information for volunteers said 'no prior experience necessary'. They accepted my application and put me through police checks.

Here I was, completely clueless but with a healthy will to learn, sitting among all the other young volunteers and waiting to be told what to do for the next fourteen days. *What have I signed up to?*

As Tim and I talked, the van shook and came to life. Our driver must have started the engine.

"Take it you've done this before," I ventured, glancing at him briefly. The van moved off the city centre car park and merged into the traffic. It would probably take over an hour to reach the Peak District where the outdoor centre we were staying in was located.

Tim grinned, showing much pride. "Yeah, this is my third summer. What about you? Are you staying for one or two weeks?"

My worries surfaced again. It'd probably be useful to talk to someone more experienced, though. "My first time, I'm afraid. I'm staying for the full fortnight camp, but I have absolutely no clue how to look after kids, let alone those with disabilities. Let's hope I don't accidentally hurt them."

Our transportation left the city centre streets behind. Tim focused back on my face again. He opened his mouth a couple of times but couldn't form the words. Finally, he smiled. "You'll be fine. I don't think physically harming them is that common."

What was left unsaid? How else could the kids be easily hurt? Crikey. Bile threatened to come up my throat.

"Anyway, Sam will sort you out," Tim concluded with conviction.

Sam. It was the first time I heard the name. I wondered who that was, but didn't want to appear ignorant or too eager. Tim sounded sure of this person's leadership. I returned to gazing out the window; I appeared like a ghost on the pane of glass: reddish-brown hair, pale eyes and a button nose. Short strands fell untidily around my oval face. I dug out my beanie and put it on to keep them under control.

The bus rolled along, taking too long to reach the hills away from the city. Even the air was thinner up there. My eyelids threatened to close as green scenery passed by. The Dark Peak was rugged and wild in parts, like a hardworking man without sentimentality. Apprehension still sat in my gut, though, as if the journey was further than the Peak District, and the hills were harbouring the unknown. I imagined the purple heather might be hiding the cloudy dreams I had as a kid when I was growing up and I'd been afraid of the strange monsters in my sleep. Now, it was waiting for me up in the hills.

The van eventually pulled into a narrow lane. Light shot through the thicket and streamed through the windows. After a mile or so, we stopped in an opening with enough space for only a few vehicles, and I saw the outdoor centre that was going to be our home for the next two weeks: a one-storey wooden structure that spread out like a resting bird; windows lined its wings that might contain the bedrooms.

Once the doors to the van opened, one by one, the helpers climbed down. I was almost the last to emerge, carrying my heavy backpack. I stood on the edge of the group, waiting to be told what was to come. Tim was deep in conversation with another young female volunteer.

The driver and her companion jumped down from the van. The first thing I noticed was the driver's legs—long and tan, strong and lean muscles stretched beneath her sports shorts. Lumberjack boots and thick socks reached her lower calves. She wore a sleeveless black T-shirt, even though it was not that hot. This was July in England, not the Mediterranean. But I found myself ogling her lithe and firm arms and thought about how the taut skin might feel if I glided my fingers along it. I had to shake my head discreetly to stop that line of thought because it was strange and as frightening as the prospect of facing the kids for the next two weeks.

The woman's head was shaved with short sides showing a tattoo just above her left ear. I was too far away to see what the tattoo was on that first day. Heat surged inside me as though I was in a hotter climate. My heart skipped a beat. I liked how she looked. A lot. I'd never had a boyfriend or girlfriend. Some of my secondary school mates were already dating. My best friend Jason was gay, so I'd gone out with him to gay clubs a few times. We'd even tracked down the only gay bookshop for miles around. We had to take a train and ride the bus to get there. But, so far, I'd thought of myself merely as an observer of Jason's world.

I'd honestly assumed I was straight. Why wouldn't I be?

"My name's Sam," the obvious leader announced. "And I'm the manager of the camp."

She related something about safety. I should've been listening to her instructions but I heard nothing but a buzz in my head.

An older guy stood by her side and introduced himself as Grant, Sam's assistant. "So, at all times, either Sam or I will be at base camp. We have two senior volunteers, Rose and Beth, who are coming with the kids in the other van. They both work in childcare, so they know their stuff. If you're in any doubt, come to one of us."

I found myself focusing on Sam. Her round face, light tan and bright brown eyes. Shit. *Pay some attention to what's being said, Josie.* I shifted in my stance to recoup. But instead of listening to Grant, I could hear birds chirp, and when I glanced to my right, I saw a squirrel running away to a clump of trees. *Deep breath.*

When I returned my attention to the two managers, I saw Sam assessing us one by one with her sharp eyes. I wasn't sure if she realised that my gaze had been following her. Her scrutiny reached me eventually, and she gave me a slight lilt of her mouth as if to wonder out loud, *who have I got here?*

I smiled back, without the same kind of confidence. We held each other's gaze for a moment. I decided then I would like her attention. No matter what. It was a far less noble motive than why I'd become a helper at a summer camp for disabled children.

Sam and Grant led us to the dormitory block. I walked side by side with Tim. The dorm was basic but clean. The scent of pine filled my nostrils as the two organisers came to a stop in the corridor flanked by several rooms. She turned to face us.

Indicating the group of dormitories, she smiled. "These are for you. You'll be sharing with another host. Ten minutes. Grant and I will be waiting for you in the hall."

Come on. She might as well have said that. Tim and I looked at each other and nodded. The others were talking, seeking out partners and inspecting the bedrooms. We grabbed the one closest to us since they were identical anyway. It was sparsely decorated, as I'd expected: two single beds, a wardrobe, a desk and chair each. Reading lamps for the occupiers. It was more than adequate for a short break. Another door led to a small bathroom with a shower stall. We dumped our bags. No time for the 'which bed would you prefer' conversation.

Tim smiled. "It ain't much but it's home for the next two weeks. Do you want to freshen up first?"

"Oh, yes. We only have ten minutes. She doesn't joke around, does she?"

"Nuh-uh. Sam runs a tight ship. Go ahead." Tim opened his backpack and pulled out some clothes to put in his wardrobe.

We had a quick wash and returned to the hall where Sam and her assistant explained that we'd ease the kids in this evening. Sam clapped her hands to draw our attention. A dozen eager faces gazed at her and her apparent leadership. Grant produced a couple of sheets of labels and some felt-tip pens.

"Everyone, pass the name tags around and write your names in big letters, so the older children can read them. Please," he instructed us.

We spent the next few minutes putting our names on the labels. As we did so, Sam added, "Of course, some of the children don't know how to read and write, but—"

She was interrupted when a timid hand was raised among the volunteers. Sam tilted her head. "Yes?"

"Do you have a list of who we're paired with?" asked a young woman with black-framed glasses and a dark short bob, and looked to be in need of summer supervision herself.

Sam read her name tag. "No, Susanna. When they arrive—" she glanced at her watch "—in a few minutes, you will simply choose one another. The children will have one-to-one supervision by their hosts at all times. It's perfectly fine, though, if you or your guest want to change during your stay, except maybe in a couple of cases because the kids can't deal with instability. Whatever it is, Grant and I will be at hand to sort things out, okay?"

With a small frown on her forehead, she looked to Grant as if to get an agreement, and he nodded.

"Some of these children have never been away from home like this. They might be emotionally challenging, as well as having physical needs. Once you've found your match, I'll have a chat with each of you individually. If you find yourself in situations you can't deal with, whatever they are, come straight to me or Grant. Understood? Any questions?" Her voice was authoritative enough that I found myself trusting her straightaway.

Grant smiled at us reassuringly. "And here's a map of the site and a list of the kids and their allocated rooms." He waved more sheets of paper and started to pass them round.

The same bespectacled young woman piped up, "What disabilities have the kids got? I don't have any experience of working with disabled children."

That made at least the two of us. I looked around, noticing several of the other volunteers nodding.

"Well, they have a wide range of disabilities, some physical, some are learning disabilities. Most of them have a mixture of both. As I said, once you've found your buddy, Grant or I will have a chat with you about individual requirements. But we don't have rigid rules here. If your guest or you feel that it's not working out, we'll try to swap you. I ask for your patience, though. Sometimes it's hard for these kids to trust people, so try to stick with them as much as possible during their stay. It *will* be fun but hard work."

At this point, I was hoping for just survival.

I squinted to see her as clearly as I could. I could see a stud in her right ear and another in her nose. The large brown eyes were deep and perfectly balanced on her face. They sparkled with enthusiasm. I was absorbed and encouraged by her unbound energy and tried to convince myself that I'd cope with whatever came my way.

Sam's phone chirped and she scanned the screen before answering. "Right. Come on in. We're ready for the guests."

I shifted my feet, still feeling nervous.

Pushing one of the kids in a wheelchair, an older woman led the group of noisy guests. I assumed she was one of the senior volunteers. Some of them were already chatting away to each other far too loudly. At first glance, they really were very different. The dozen children were of different sizes, ages and genders.

The guests, too, had name labels on their lapels but I was too distant to read them. After all the kids had entered the hall, a woman about Sam's age brought up the rear. Sam introduced them; Rose was the older woman, and the younger senior helper was Beth. I was reassured since, according to Sam, they were both trained in caring for disabled children.

I surveyed the kids. My eyes were drawn to a couple of boys who stood awkwardly to one end of the group. They were both taller than me. One of them might have been a teenager but he already had an adult's body, and yet, one side of him drooped. His right arm and leg were bent and his pale face blank. He stared at us, the helpers. Saliva drooled from the corner of his mouth.

With a mop of messy curly brown hair, the boy standing at the very end of the group was probably a little younger than his neighbour, but he also appeared tall for his age. He didn't seem physically disabled, unlike the teenager next to him. He shifted slightly backwards, as if he wanted to get away from the line-up, and glanced up momentarily. His eyes were so large and deep, clear blue like two pools of tarn. He caught my gaze and quickly directed his eyes down, away from my scrutiny. I felt bad, as though I was staring too much. Later, he'd teach me that most people over-compensated all the time. They deliberately looked away from physical disability or behaviour that seemed out of the ordinary. He would catch on anyway when they did that. For him, over-compensation was a sign that 'the real people'—his words for the able-bodied—were scared.

I'm scared of them, but not as much as they are frightened of us freaks.

And I would ask him not to use that word to describe himself. He smiled at that with a slight upturn of his mouth. Then, standing awkwardly in that hall, I had no clue what I was doing, and wondered why the boy had come to the camp because he didn't look like the rest of the gang of kids.

For now, he avoided eye contact and leaned uncomfortably, one hand holding onto his bag so tightly that I saw his white knuckles from ten feet away. All I could remember was the parent dabbing her eyes, trying to will away her worries. She might be his mum, and now he wanted to show her he was a big independent boy who was not scared to death.

I was not alone in feeling nervous. I took comfort in that thought.

"Come on, why don't our hosts pair up with the guests? One-to-one. My lovely helpers, you may show them where their bunks are. All the allocations are shown on the plan we gave you." Sam, as ever, sounded excited and enthusiastic and stopped my wandering train of thought.

The other volunteers went up and started to 'claim' their companions. The hosts and guests eagerly greeted each other, some striking up conversations right away. Tim went to the tall teenager whose twisted leg dragged along as Tim made his introductions and led him to the dormitories.

The remaining boy flapped his hands and moved away even more, as if he was making for the door he'd just come through to escape. He shook his head and muttered something to no one in particular. While he waited in absolute agony and I hesitated, all the other children and volunteers had made their acquaintances and, one by one, the pairs disappeared.

Rose and Beth had left with them to offer assistance. Sam wasn't in the room anymore. Only Grant hovered, ready to lend a hand.

I moved towards the last boy standing. He still held onto his bag tightly with his eyes downcast, avoiding my gaze.

"I'm Josie. What's your name?"

I extended my hand to shake his while I tried to read his name label and saw that he'd written his name in rather small letters in the left-hand corner of the white rectangle. The handwriting was neat and controlled, but I couldn't read it. Except the 'L'.

My offered hand remained untouched.

"What's your name?" he replied without meeting my eyes or returning my handshake. His speech was clear. Words pronounced in imitation of my accent.

I hesitantly moved closer and was now near enough to see his name: Lucian. The letters were drawn in a tight script that broke the white surface.

I didn't know what might be considered wrong about him by society, but my instinct told me we'd be fine. That we'd make this work. "Would you like to pair up with me, Lucian?"

I smiled because at that time I still believed if I did that enough I would gain people's trust. Except, Lucian was exceptional. He failed to look up to meet my smile and he didn't respond.

I was at a loss as to how to act in front of the teenager. Nothing in my eighteen years of experience prepared me for understanding differences. I considered him again. He appeared like any other boy of his age and yet in that simple rejection betrayed an innate distinction.

As I pondered upon his disability, he flapped his hand once more and pointed to the sheet of names and room arrangement, still without meeting my gaze. I held it up and read through the list of names and in which room he was allocated.

I'd already withdrawn my hand since it had become quite clear he was not going to touch me. I offered instead, "Okay, Lucian. Shall I take you to your room?"

I realised that he'd have known that I held the information in my hand. He would have deduced that fact because of his ability to observe and remember the minutiae.

He risked a glance at my face, his blue eyes glistening. He nodded and started for the door. Instead of being the host, I had to follow his long legs and head towards the corridor where the children's rooms were found.

We marched past the room he was to share with two other guests.

"Hey, this one. Here." I puffed, holding onto the map.

Lucian's bunk sat empty in one corner. The other volunteers and children were chatting away. Lucian approached his space. Immediately, he took his possessions from his bag and arranged them in the small wardrobe and on the desk. His colouring pencils were neatly ordered in the rainbow colours they came in, and I could see he'd sharpened them to equal length. I watched him carefully claiming his personal space with fascination.

"How old are you, Lucian?"

"How old are you?" he countered, without directly addressing me. "Why don't you look at your sheet?"

I found him on my list. *Lucian Charles. Fifteen.*

Damn it. He was making me feel like an idiot, which was precisely his plan. Lucian had probably been treated like one his entire life. Now he was taking me for a fool. Perfect.

What I could deduce after my first evening with Lucian: he didn't like crowds. He liked to stick to a schedule. Minimum eye contact when he interacted with others. He put everything in order, including food.

By my own bedtime, I was exhausted from trying to be on form all day.

DAY 2

L UCIAN KNEW EXACTLY what he wanted from the breakfast bar. He'd arranged the egg cup in the very centre of his plate. The beans sat to the left, a single sausage next to the tomato sauce. A small plate held the piece of toast to the right. Still not speaking to me, he was happy enough with the meal, finishing everything meticulously. I wondered if someone made a mistake to let Lucian onto this camp since he appeared capable enough. For a start, he didn't need feeding like some of the other kids.

Lucian took a sip of the orange juice and stuck his tongue out. "Disgusting." He pushed the drink as far away from him as possible, as though it might contaminate the rest of the meal. If that was his only complaint, I thought we were doing great.

Sam caught up with me when Lucian had nearly finished breakfast. "Rose could sit with Lucian for the moment. Would you like to come with me to the office? We'll have a chat."

Oh, the honeyed tone. It went with the brown eyes. Sam wore a plain black T-shirt and a pair of cutoff shorts. Her body was harder and leaner than most women I knew. I stared, as if hypnotised, and I stood up and followed her into the office. The small room was sparsely furnished. It wasn't somewhere that was used constantly. Sam sat behind the narrow desk and I took the seat opposite. The two feet of wood between us added to my anxiety.

She launched into it without pleasantry as preparation. "How's it going with Lucian?"

Feeling oddly tongue-tied, I mumbled, "Fine, I think."

Sam arched an eyebrow, which might have betrayed how she felt uncertain about my ability. Did I seem like a useless kid who needed guidance? I wished I had more confidence about the whole situation.

"Fine? How do you find him?" Impatience permeated her question.

"He…he is intense. Kind of quiet. It's too early yet." *Lucian is odd, intriguing, not particularly communicative.* I couldn't say any of it. It'd seem too much like I was complaining about the disabled kid whom I was supposed to be taking care of.

"Lucian has autism spectrum disorder," she advised me.

I racked my brains to see whether I knew anything about autism. Sam's dark gaze made me give up. "What do you mean? What should I expect?"

Sam waited moments as if she was measuring out the words. "It's hard to tell. From my experience, every autistic kid's quite unique. I don't know where he is on the spectrum. Some of them can be 'highly functional'." She made the quotation marks in the air. "I don't like the term. It makes them sound like flipping robots. Some call the condition Asperger's syndrome. As you've seen, they can be anxious in social situations. They need familiar routine and order. I've worked with Lucian before. He's pretty good at looking after himself."

"He just seems a bit peculiar," I ventured. After only brief encounters with Lucian last night and this morning, I'd only say he wasn't particularly 'dysfunctional'. Perhaps that was why Tim went for the other boy whose name was Eric and who was certainly much higher maintenance.

"It's your first time at these camps, right? Lucian's probably not a bad guest to be teamed with."

Sam was distracting me. Under the tight T-shirt, her small breasts and the shape of her nipples were barely visible. My mind had instantly deserted me.

"He seems particularly anxious, which is not surprising. His mum seldom lets him out of her sight, I think. He's been here the last couple of years," Sam continued. Lucian was nervous, but perhaps no more than I was. "He doesn't relate well to the other kids and the helpers. He's a stickler for routine. No doubt you'll find out for yourself. Some involuntary hand and head gestures, and repetitive speech pattern. It's called echolalia."

I was staring, mesmerised by Sam's voice, but the list of Lucian's 'symptoms' washed over me because they sounded like a biology lesson.

As though she could hear my thoughts, she added, "But other than that, Lucian's a great kid. You'll probably get on. I have a feeling."

Once more, I asked myself what I was doing there, but Sam's laughter broke through the tension. After a minute, she was still chuckling. "You are staring with your mouth open. Lucian wouldn't look you in the eyes. You will make a great pair."

I felt like a fool, again, pretending that I could look after someone not much younger than me. Someone who had special needs, which I must provide for. I must have blushed.

Sam gave me one more wide beam. "Humour. Above all, you need some of that. Otherwise, he's going to run rings around you, my love. And working with these kids is hard work. It can be emotionally draining."

I was serious. I'd been told many times about that particular personality trait, and Sam's pep talk had not eased my apprehension one bit. I still felt the warmth on my cheeks.

She clapped her hands to signal the end of the conversation. "The kids are doing the great escape this morning. Ha, it's only the second day and they're trying to get away already. Come on. Let's go see." She stood, came round to my side of the desk and offered me her hand. Her long, slender fingers touched mine, and the next thing I knew I was standing, our palms together.

Sam dropped my hand, then, winked and ran ahead. I thought if I stared at her any more my eyes would pop out. Instead, I followed her and found the others out the back of the camp where the adventure playground was.

Complex climbing frames and rope structures dominated the middle of the field. A zip wire and balance beam stood to the side. Most of the kids were crawling inside the rope tube. Two of the centre staff were shouting instructions to them, while the volunteers and children who were waiting for their turns cheered on those currently in action.

I scanned the area looking for Lucian and found him, squeezed into a corner as far away from the others as possible.

Under the natural shade of a bush, he sat cross-legged, his baseball cap low, and he was reading.

I sat next to him. The novel in his hands was dog-eared and tatty. After a few minutes, he took off his hat, and re-focused on the page, frowning with a deep V in his forehead as he read.

"Why aren't you doing the activity?" I instinctively knew the reason but I wanted to engage him in conversation.

His attention didn't shift from the words. "I am too big to get through the nets. And. It's my reading time."

I wondered. He was lanky for his age. Would he prefer to be doing something else, going on holiday somewhere more exotic? Most boys of his age might be out with their friends. It was the summer after all.

Instead of asking about that, I ventured, "What are you reading? Do you like it?"

He showed me a Philip K. Dick novel, then in his most deadpanned way, he answered, "No. I hate reading and I hate the books I read."

No laughter. Not quite irony. *I need a fucking sense of humour.* It would certainly seem odd to most people if they didn't know Lucian because he wasn't smiling and showing that this was a joke.

"I watch films I hate again and again, too." I could see a slight lilt of Lucian's mouth, just for a fleeting moment before he went back to his book and ignored me.

I remained on the damp grass, keeping Lucian company, and watched the kids having fun, letting their hair down. I remembered the guidance from the brochure, and Sam and Grant: the holiday camp was for the children, not the volunteers. So, it wasn't up to me to force Lucian to try anything.

Eric and Tim were playing in the nearby playground. Coordinating his movements for the ropes would have been too much for Eric, and, like Lucian, he was too big for some of the equipment. Lucian didn't once talk to me again. By the time the activity finished, he had read half of the thin paperback. I thought the fact that we'd shared comfortable silence meant that I'd penetrated his hard shell. Sam suggested that Lucian wasn't difficult to deal with.

I couldn't be more wrong.

At lunch, I led Lucian to the restaurant. The noise hit us first as we entered the dining room. We were the last to arrive. The volunteers and the kids talked animatedly. The senior helpers and the cook were bringing out the food. Sounds vibrated and echoed between the wood floor and the slatted ceiling.

A few steps into the lunch hall, Lucian stopped and stared at the scene in front of him. His feet refused to move, and his right hand flapped. Always the right hand.

"Hey, it's okay. We can sit in the corner." I talked softly as though I was compensating for the noises.

I could tell Lucian had to stop himself from bolting. We walked over to the corner, even though there was still little privacy. Lucian waited until all the others had got their lunch before asking for a plate of chips and sweetcorn. I went up to the serving hatch and conveyed his order, asking for the same and a bowl of green salad for myself.

As we ate, I tried to start a conversation with him. "So, Sam told me you came to the camp last year as well. You must like it."

His hand stilled and he frowned. "My mum needed a break."

No, I don't love it here. I can't stand you all, and please don't pretend to be friendly.

I, somehow, understood all of that except how to deal with it. So, we lapsed into silence once more and ate our lunch.

He concentrated on the food and refused to make eye contact. The scowl on his face never left, though. I must have reminded him that he missed home. *Shit.*

It was hard to tell how he was feeling.

Lucian arranged the chips in rows, pushed to the top left of the plate. The sweetcorn proved a challenge. They were not behaving and staying in the bottom right corner. He struggled a little with the fork and the chips, then he reached out to the bowl of salad, which meant crossing in front of me.

I made a fatal mistake in my attempt to 'help' Lucian. I grabbed his hand. Mine was too cold, but against his slim digits, it felt like burning.

"It's okay. Let me put some on your plate."

But he didn't stop. He desperately tried to reach the leaves; our joined hands hovered above the bowl.

"Let me help you. You want some salad, right?"

"Salad, right."

I took it as a cue to take the fork from his hand. Leaning too close, I tightened on his hand with the fork. "Let me, it's okay."

But he didn't let go of my hand. Instead, he jerked away, switched the fork to his other hand. A sharp pain cut through the back of mine and travelled up my arm. He'd stabbed me with the fork, momentarily pinning my hand to the table. A couple of drops of blood oozed out of the back of my hand. I stared at the wound, unsure how long I was still like that. I must have whimpered. I didn't scream because it'd looked worse than it was. I couldn't feel much pain.

I looked up, and Lucian was watching my hand.

The unruly sweetcorn escaped from the plate and scattered on the floor.

I was aware of Lucian but nothing else, as though we were in a bubble. It was almost peaceful. I couldn't sense the other people in the dining hall at all. Lucian shook his head violently.

I gradually came back to reality, as I could hear rather than see the commotion around us. One of the young girls at the next table, Anna, saw what had happened and she was now screaming. Lucian covered his ears. He stood up, pushing his chair back and trying to shield himself from the distress call by hiding under the table and behind the chair.

Tim and Sam immediately came forward. They stood there while I felt hopeless. I turned around and realised that the other children were horrified and staring. Anna's host hurriedly led her out of the dining room. Sam asked the other pairs to go back to the children's bedrooms, too, so they could take a nap before the afternoon's activities. The kids were curious and some remained focused on us as they departed from the room.

Tim took my hand and inspected the wound. I had little flesh there, so Lucian had only managed to prick the surface of the skin. Even though Anna's scream had ceased, Lucian stayed behind the chair and he started to mumble to himself.

Sam held out her arms as though she was trying to surrender. "Lucian, it's okay. Would you like to go back to your room? Let Tim take you, okay?"

He peered out from under the table. He clutched his chest, and inhaled and exhaled, as if he was hyperventilating, but he managed to stop himself after several minutes. Sam used her eyes to plead for help. Tim came forward and gestured for Lucian to follow.

Sam knelt down. "It's okay. Come on out."

Lucian climbed out slowly and followed Tim. For the first time, he held my gaze, and I could tell he was trying to say sorry. His quickened exhales were beginning to ease. Finally he dropped his head and exited the dining room behind Tim.

Sam smiled calmly, and for the second time in two days, she took my hand—the good one. The back of the other was a little raised and swollen. She led me down the quiet corridor to the small medical room.

It was stuffy in the room, and I was conscious of our close proximity as she sat me on the patient's chair and leaned over me to inspect the back of my hand. Her warm arm touched mine, our hands linked.

I flinched not because of the touch, but the tingling I felt in my groin. My hand should be feeling, not anywhere else in my body. She bent down further to have a look at my wound. I closed my eyes and smelled her: the faint sweat and a grassy kind of scent. I loved that it was earthy rather than feminine. And I found myself inhaling, trying to remember her that way. When I opened my eyes, I saw her brown irises looking right back at me, assessing my face rather than the small stab wound.

I might have noticed the lust in her gaze but my self-doubt asked if I was misinterpreting. My wishful thinking. Perhaps my sweat could be translated as a natural reaction to the non-existent heat of a British summer.

"He hit the bone. Does it hurt?" She dropped my hand to look for the first-aid kit, removing her body heat. *No, come back. Never mind the first-aid kit.*

"Not really." It throbbed a little at first but I'd been thoroughly distracted.

Sam approached me again, and opened the first-aid box and wiped my wound—the reddened flesh—with saline lotion. Her head bowed in front of my chest. Her faint scent filled my nostrils once again.

Then I remembered a similar scene when I fell over during sports day at school and my good friend Ginnie had come with me to the medical room. She even cried with worry. We were close, and I'd marvelled at her beautiful round brown eyes, fat teardrops and freckles, and my insides swelled. Ginnie had smelt of something sweet and fragrant. We were eleven. I had not thought of Ginnie after she moved away to Australia. But as Sam was patching up my hand, the memory came back to me.

Sam seemed to know what she was doing with the sterilising and she finished with a plaster. "If you feel anything unusual. It starts hurting bad, anything like that. You need to tell me right away. I'll take you to A and E."

I nodded. It didn't hurt, and even if it did, I couldn't blame Lucian.

"Will Lucian be okay?" I whispered. I didn't want him to be sent home.

Sam lifted her eyes to meet mine. "Of course. You?"

"Yes. I'm fine. Lucian would love to go home, though. Sorry, I fucked up."

She shook her head. "I'm not sure if his mum will be okay with that. And, you haven't messed up. Believe me."

I'd only been there a day. I'd already failed the boy I was supposed to care for, and my insides were still trembling as Sam held onto my hand. The dull pain was long forgotten. Instead, I was embarrassed and aroused in a mess of warring emotions.

I avoided her eyes. It was easier that way. There was so much I wanted to ask her, needed to ask her, but I didn't. I'd do nothing and wait for the two weeks to be over. I'd tell myself that it was a silly crush and nothing more. We all had our lives outside of this, and hers would certainly exclude me. Yet, I knew she would impart the wisdom that I was to be convinced of, and I wanted to hear it.

Becoming eighteen was supposed to be a sign of childhood passing, but what I'd learn about myself in fourteen days would somehow turn all previous years of socialisation upside down, as though I had been stripped of my adult status, and rebuilt.

As if Sam knew that already, she pulled away and ruffled my hair as though I were a child. I wore it short. The red strands hung over us. I could never grow it out. Instead of looking like a pre-Raphaelite beauty, I usually ended up as if I had a giant orange over my head.

"Remember, if anything changes, you need to come to me right away." She looked the most serious I'd seen her yet.

"All right."

"You're okay to carry on tomorrow? Tim can swap with you, if you want?" she asked tentatively.

No, I wasn't going to regret being Lucian's helper. I was even more determined to get it right.

"I'm staying with Lucian if he'll let me." I smiled.

DAY 3

I WOKE EVERY DAY as if I was waiting for a date, needing to get up, see to my charge, and impress the hell out of Sam. I found myself trying to catch her attention. I didn't even know if she liked girls, let alone a young inexperienced one like me. She often caught me watching her when she was speaking to another volunteer or organising the activities, and she would smile at me. Her grin lit up her face and made my heart flutter.

I couldn't stop myself from thinking about her. From that point of view, it was going to be two very long weeks.

Lucian was a good distraction. He was, in fact, the perfect partner in crime, making me use all my senses differently and forget about my Sam obsession.

After breakfast on our third day, Lucian ran back into his room and sat on his bunk, burying his head in his hands. "No! No! That wasn't in the timetable you showed me."

All the activities were planned in advance. Lucian had already seen the timetable and decided whether he would participate or not. He also had his own schedule.

Sam and I followed him but kept our distance away from his bed. Sam tried to placate him. "We have to change the schedule because it's raining, darling."

Sam and Grant had decided to change the planned outdoor activity due to the weather. Big drops of rain were hitting the wood structure, like a few bars of staccato. The air felt damp. I stared at the water-soaked windows.

Lucian lifted his eyes and gazed at us for a moment, his irises large with indignation but his words steady as always, showing conviction in his stubbornness. "I won't go to an indoor play centre."

They were driving the kids away from camp so they could use the indoor frames, slides and ball pools. I had to agree that it was not really an appropriate option for him because he was too tall and too old, though Eric was going to come with us anyway and he'd probably have a drink and lunch while the younger kids played. I could do that with Lucian, but I also understood why he was reluctant. I imagined that a confined space full of screaming and running kids was not Lucian's thing. Sam and I looked at each other. She arched an eyebrow like a question mark.

"I… I could stay with Lucian," I offered despite what had happened last night. Lucian might not want me to, though.

Sam hesitated. "Lucian?"

He flapped his hand and averted his eyes after stealing a glance at me. No objection from Lucian was as good as a 'yes' since he wasn't usually shy about his demands.

Sam considered me for long moments and nodded. "Okay. Grant can stay behind, too, if you need him. I'll take Rose and Beth." She gazed intently at Lucian again. "Lucian, you'll be good, yeah?"

He stared at his feet with the same blankness and did not reply. Sam tilted her head, so I followed her out.

Once we were away from Lucian's room and his earshot, we stopped and Sam turned to speak to me. "To be honest, a play centre would overwhelm him. Are you happy with this? Honestly. I'm sure Grant can deal with him, and you can come with us to Tumbleweed."

I nodded. "Come on! I'm getting used to him. Even another fork incident wouldn't be that bad." I smiled, amused by my mockery.

Sam grinned at my little joke. "Ha! Come on. Don't you get another injury. I have to write a stupid report every time something like that happens."

I was oddly confident about my ability to cope with Lucian. I didn't know why. It was as though Lucian stabbing me with a fork meant his heart was open to me now. I couldn't care less that he'd hurt me. I touched my chin with that same hand; I'd put a fresh plaster on the spot this morning.

"Well, good luck with it. Don't hesitate to get Grant to call me," Sam said at the end. She turned abruptly. I watched her strong back as she left, and exhaled.

When I returned to Lucian's room, he was reading his book.

I sat on the chair by his bed. "What would you like to do today, Lucian?"

He didn't look up from his book. "It's Tuesday. I draw in the morning."

"Okay. Let's get your art materials out, then."

He put his book down and carefully slotted a bookmark.

I took his bag from under the bunk, but he snatched it back without meeting my eyes. He brought out colour pencils, a pencil case, a pad of paper and placed them in a neat arrangement on the narrow desk. The pencils lined up tidily in their rainbow colour range, and the paper sat squarely on the flat surface. He used a ruler and the pencils to draw sixteen rectangles—two rows with eight each. He took out a yellow pencil and filled in the boxes except one. The room was quiet except for our breaths and the sharpened colour pencil tips that danced across the paper, making a scratchy sound.

"What are they?" I was curious.

Lucian raised his eyes and, as if he'd seen me for the first time, his pupils dilated. "Lights."

"Lights?"

"You're repeating what I said, and yes." He breathed out, as if exasperated by my ignorance.

"Lights, yes." Repetition felt good. It really did.

"The lights in the main hall. Two columns and eight shades in each."

I scrutinised his picture again. It was meticulously drawn. If I stopped thinking about the rectangles as shapes, I could see them from Lucian's perspective. I had never thought to look up, to see what kinds of lights there were. I closed my eyes and tried to remember the warm glow from them.

When I opened my eyes again, the afterglow of the yellow had imprinted in my mind's eye. I pointed to the blank one. "Why is that one different from the others?"

Lucian's head covered the drawing as he concentrated. "It broke. On the day we arrived, it flickered. Then it stopped working. It should be fixed." The grave tone in his voice said it was an important issue.

Imperfection. It made sense. None of us would have noticed something so small, but it was beautiful. If it was important to him, then it was not trivial.

"What else do you like looking at? Do you count anything else?"

"Lots of things need fixing. The loudspeakers there. They are not balanced. The one on the right-hand side hangs sideways, so it sounds wrong. No one cared when they played the movie last night." He delivered this piece of information with authority, his voice steady.

When he finished the first drawing, he tore out another blank sheet and drew the lights again, slowly, moving the ruler and the angle of the sheet systematically. After he finished the rectangles, he filled them out with the yellow again, making sure that it stayed within the lines.

Before meeting Lucian, I'd thought I was impulsive and sometimes too twitchy, but he taught me patience, to sit for hours, working in repetition. I would spend some of those hours writing stories or reading books. I read my tales later and found them unbearably childish, but they reminded me of Lucian and that summer. My heart would ache for the innocence.

"Tell me more about the lights." I couldn't help it. He'd made me care about them as much as he did.

He never broke his concentration but continued to draw and colour. "I like them."

At some point, I looked up from my book to catch Lucian with his eyes closed and his head tilted.

"You okay?" I asked.

Lucian didn't answer for a while but his eyelids fluttered. Finally, he asked me a question instead. "What can you hear?"

I copied him and closed my eyes. It was quiet since all the kids and volunteers had gone. Grant was probably in the office. At first, I only heard our breaths, but I persevered. The rain pattered on the window and the wood of the building. The sounds were different, more vibrant than any rainfall I'd heard before. At intervals, they were muted. Lucian hadn't said a word.

I thought Lucian was pulling my leg, one of his quirky things, but then something changed. My consciousness took me away. It was as if I was transposed outside in the damp. Birds were chattering despite the rain. Tree branches swayed in the breeze. The rain and wind increased their velocity like a crescendo before they retreated again. When the wind pelted the raindrops hard against the windows, the sounds were like small hammers on a dulcimer.

When the rain eased for a few moments, I'd hear a distant bark. The gust picked up once more, howling through the structure of the centre. I couldn't tell how long Lucian and I had been listening to the symphony of nature.

I didn't open my eyes until Lucian spoke. "You heard them, then?"

I nodded.

Lucian's pencils glided across the drawing. When he did glance at me, it was as if he saw through me. "Most people can't. All they hear is the noise they make themselves."

I was mesmerised by that idea, and his ordered picture.

"What do your schoolmates think about the stuff you draw?"

He stopped to sharpen the yellow pencil. "I don't go to school."

Two days with Lucian and I'd almost forgotten that we were in a camp for disabled children. Lucian had abilities that were not exactly valued by most people. And most schools wanted to teach kids who were cardboard cutouts. Kids were often little tyrants who would taunt anyone who didn't belong, and pick on those weaker than them. I must have stared at him. 'Sorry' nearly escaped my mouth but I kept mum because it seemed like the wrong word.

"My mum home-schools me." Something else clicked into my information bank about Lucian. I imagined his mother working hard to teach him at home, protecting him from harm. It probably explained why she needed a break and how Lucian felt abandoned being sent to a summer camp and forced to be befriended by a bunch of strangers.

I wondered why he was home-schooled; perhaps I'd asked him out loud.

"When I was eleven, some boys thought it was funny to laugh at me." He raised his right hand and tilted his head towards the window and the sky beyond, his fingers drawing in the air. "My mum was late collecting me one day, and they hurt me."

His hand stalled and it started to shake. I wanted to hug him, but this time I knew better.

Instead, I asked quietly, "What happened?"

His eyelids fluttered once more. Still half-facing the clouds outside, he mumbled, hardly audibly, "They hit me and took my trousers down and…"

"Did they hurt you?" I wasn't sure if I should ask him what they tried to do when they took his pants down. I had no right to ask him to re-live something bad for my benefit, but I was too concerned to stop myself from asking the question.

For a few seconds, I wasn't sure if he'd answer, but he did.

"I beat them up. This boy Simon."

I was worried about him. I wouldn't expect that he was the one who hurt the bullies. *Was he quick to respond, to stand up for himself? Like he did last night?*

"I broke his teeth and I hurt him pretty bad. They had to take him to the hospital. After that, they said I had to go to a special school and Mum didn't want me to go, so she looks after me at home." As he explained it to me, he started drawing another picture of the lights.

I could visualise the scene. He wasn't small in stature and he'd be strong when provoked. The indignation of the bully. The school put in an impossible position. His mum's protectiveness. I stared at the teenager for long moments. *How do you feel about it all, Lucian?*

That night I flopped onto my bed exhausted. I observed Tim reading under the weak lamp.

"I'm so knackered." A big yawn escaped despite myself.

He gazed over the top edge of his paperback. "Yeah, well. Coping with the emotional engagement is hard. At least you don't have the physical stuff to deal with." He was referring to Eric.

I agreed. I'd come into this rather blind, so the reality shocked me.

Tim put a bookmark in his novel. "Did you say you're the youngest in the family?"

"Yeah. I've got an older brother." He was a couple of years older than me, but we didn't exactly get on. Just like my mum, he left me alone unless he had something smartass to say to me. I mostly kept myself to myself at home.

His intelligent eyes assessed me. "Then, you don't even have experience of looking after younger siblings."

"No. But, I'm not surprised that the kids' parents need some time off." I thought of the woman who cried at the beginning of the camp, tearing up when she saw her child going off without her. "Caring for Lucian is tiring, but I feel guilty for thinking it."

"Don't be. It's only natural."

I smiled. "Thanks."

"It's definitely more working than holiday. Do you like it, though? Think you'll come back next year?"

"Hmm. Ask me again after this ends, or a few months down the line." It was a life-changing experience, but I didn't know if I'd repeat it next year. My future was wide open.

Tim laughed, his shoulders shaking with amusement. "Yeah. I was absolutely horrified at first, and swore I'd never do this again. Here I am three years later, happily wiping Eric's bottom."

I chuckled, too, a little impishly. I'd seen Tim clean Eric up because he had to wear incontinence pads. I was uncomfortable about it at first, but after a couple of days here, I'd begun to get used to the kids. I no longer thought of them as strange and vulnerable.

"You okay?" Tim asked.

"Yeah, why?"

He winced. "I've seen Lucian during previous years' camps. He has a foul temper, for sure. I know it's part of his condition, but none of his helpers before were able to deal with it, or stay with him. Sam had to keep changing his partners. But, you seem happy. You get on with Lucian and…"

I chuckled. "What? Even with the fork incident?"

Tim laughed. "It's just a meltdown. Believe me, I've seen him in a much worse state. He's more grown up this year. You're doing great."

The compliment was ego boosting, but I was still wary of a repeat of Lucian's meltdown. "It's early days. I don't want to jinx it."

"No, you don't."

"Why have you volunteered?" *And kept at it.*

Tim cocked his head as if deciding whether he'd tell me. "I like working with children. I'm doing my teacher training, and this is extra experience." He paused for moments. I waited for him to continue.

"My mum died when I was thirteen."

"I'm sorry," I offered.

Tim raised his hand to accept my very belated condolence. "It's ten years ago. I'm an only child. My dad seems to have decided not to date or remarry. We had help, though, from relatives, friends, good teachers. That's what made me believe it's important to give to children as much as we can, in whichever capacity we can."

I nodded. It made sense.

Tim continued, "I'm gay. So, I reckon I'm not going to have kids in the traditional way. I love helping them grow. I want to work with them, and volunteer in my spare time." The sparkle in his eyes filled me with joy. If all our teachers felt the same, we'd have a nation of happy kids.

I smiled. "That's so cool. I wish I had as much conviction as you."

Tim chuckled. "You're here. You're doing a good thing." He raised his hand again, this time to high-five me. I obliged.

"Maybe you can adopt?" I suggested.

Tim smiled. "Yeah. I think I'll find a good partner first. You know how much work raising kids is now."

He went back to his book for a few minutes while I wrote in my diary. I wondered whether I should ask him. I was intrigued and he obviously knew the working of these camps well.

"What do you think of Sam?" I tried to sound as casual as I could.

He hesitated, putting down his book yet again. There was something he wasn't saying. Tim was only a few years older than me, but he'd finished university, was training to be a teacher and had volunteered with Sam before. Eventually, he breathed out. "Sam. She's enigmatic, for sure."

He uttered those words like a warning. I hated the feeling of being too young and innocent to comprehend caution, but I was already far too infatuated.

I had glimpses of evidence that I ignored. Sam talking on the mobile to someone, standing away from the crowd, listening and speaking in a hushed voice. Her face seemed serious, different from how she was with the kids and how she talked to me.

DAY 4

I T SEEMED THAT every day was a struggle against Lucian's sensibility.

After an hour in the pool, the kids were going to tackle the maze, but Lucian declared he had to do writing. *It's in my schedule.* He felt unable to join in many of the activities, but most of the time it was because the other kids were too noisy. They were far too much stimulation for Lucian.

I managed to persuade him to take his notebook and write outside, so at least we were sitting near the group. The sun had returned and we were set to have great weather for the rest of the time. I sat next to him, watching the kids get lost in the maze through the tint of my sunglasses, with the warm sun touching my bare skin.

Lucian hunched over and wrote in small controlled letters. His writing was extremely neat, but he liked to confine himself to the corner of the page, no matter how big the white space was. This morning, he was filling up the pages of a bound notebook.

"What are you writing?"

"My diary." He didn't look up. "My mum will read it. I'm telling her what we've been doing here."

I knew better than to remind him that he wasn't at home, so I avoided talking about how she might have missed him. "What've you written so far?"

He took so long to answer, I thought he wasn't going to. His head bowed low, he quietly responded at the end, "I told her I had one meltdown, and I hurt this lady. I won't do it again."

35

His apology. I didn't expect one but it was good to hear it. Tears pricked the back of my eyes. I could only whisper, "Thank you."

Lucian continued to scribble, but I saw him glance at my injured hand. So I suggested, "Do you want to touch it?"

He waited a few beats. "Okay." His fingers reached out and they ghosted my hand. Our skin connected, and the touch magnified in importance. All around us, laughter of the children drifted and filled the air with a renewed optimism.

But life for Lucian did seem a long string of challenges. The kitchen made a fatal mistake by changing the lunch menu because they ran out of one ingredient or another. He stared at the gooey beef stew and a lasagne.

"Only pizza, chips, sweetcorn and macaroni cheese, tomato sauce with no bits, mash, Quorn sausages. I put them on my form." Lucian's arms were crossed in front of his chest, protecting and protesting. He wore his trademark frown. I gazed at Rose and Beth who were helping to dish up the food, but we all felt hopeless in the situation.

Sam came forward. "Lucian, we have spaghetti and meatballs tonight. I promise we will have one of those things for you tomorrow."

"The tomato sauce has green bits in it." His face was pinched. This was a serious problem.

"It's basil," Beth offered meekly.

"I don't eat that."

I intervened, my protective host persona taking over. "Would you like some bread? Tomorrow, I'll make sure they cook something you'll eat." I glanced at Sam, appealing for her help. *Whatever you do, sort him out.*

Lucian shifted his feet. He behaved as though he was sulking, and yet his facial expression was rather bland except the V between his eyebrows. He was more perplexed and frustrated than angry. It was difficult for him to accept what a disorder the world was in. I recognised his traits now. Many of the other kids had stopped eating and stared at him, wondering if they should have a complaint, too.

Eventually, he uttered, "Okay."

I put the bread and butter on his plate. He walked over to his corner and sat down, while I tried to hide a sigh.

Sam smiled at me and whispered in my ear, "I'll personally drive to the village store and cook him the damn meals if it causes such disruption." She then strolled off.

I grinned at her departing form. During those days, I seemed to be obsessed with nothing but parts of her: the dark eyes, tan and taut skin, the boldness of her speech. My heart sang when she was around, and my eyes automatically searched for her whenever I entered a room. It was a crush or something incurable.

For the rest of the time, alongside Lucian, I had to be grown up and responsible. Hell, the kids' parents had to be desperate enough to let us look after them at the camp. But no judgement. I'd never know what permanently living with a teenager like Lucian would be like. If I were his mother or maybe big sister, I'd love him so much and want to be there no matter what. And it'd hurt seeing how he struggled to fit in.

He ate his bread quickly and drank the milk, stealing glances at me or some part of me anyway as he always avoided people's faces. I was getting used to Lucian and all his quirks as though I'd known him for some time.

The guests tended to go to bed early. By nine, they'd have all disappeared to their bunks. Lucian would go to his room and read.

The evenings were time for ourselves, time to relax and unwind.

It was close to midnight. Sometimes the children used it during the day, but at this time of the night the swimming pool was usually quiet. Tonight, I'd come particularly late, having impulsively decided to have a late swim. I came out of the changing room, gripping my towel, and trotted along while my flip-flops made a plop-plop noise. The chlorine smelt strong. The fluorescent tubes were too bright, bathing the cavernous room with blues and greens.

The splashing of water caught my attention first. A lone figure was there gliding through the lanes.

Sam wore a black one piece that showed off her shapely body. She was swimming freestyle; her movements were powerful even though she wasn't perfect in her strokes. Water parted around her as she came up for breaths. Her body stretched and glided along in between the waves. I stared, mesmerised, forgetting that I'd been motionless by the steps.

Drops of water turned sparkly, clinging to her golden skin as if they were jewels. I was paralysed from the potency of the image. When I realised I'd been gazing at her for too long, I gingerly moved to enter the pool. She glanced up, taking her goggles off and soaking up my physique in return. Instead of feeling self-conscious, it felt as though this was natural, that our bodies should announce themselves to each other.

I smiled and let my skin acclimatise to the slight chill of the pool water.

Sam grinned at me. "It's one of the best things about this camp. You're the first person who's come to swim this late at night, though. I normally have the whole place to myself."

"Sorry to disturb your peace."

"Nah. I'm nearly finished. Go ahead." She turned, secured her goggles and was off again. I followed.

Sam left after completing a couple more lengths. I'd forgotten about the strokes because all I could think about was her lithe body like a big fish, possessing the water. I nearly choked and came up for air, just in time to see her pushing open the door into the showers.

DAY 5

I CLIMBED ONTO THE driver's seat of the van. The plaster on the back of my hand was a reminder of what Lucian had done. No doubt Sam had taken me along for the ride to give me a break from caring for him, from the intensity of being there for someone this way. I felt like I'd known the boy for five years not four days, and yet, he was as opaque to me as the black shade on the window. Something had been changing, though, between Lucian and me. His body language said so. We didn't always need to talk, touch or make eye contact. There were other means of communication and he was teaching me his ways. I closed my eyes and listened, tuning into the cacophony of sounds, some noisier, some no more than whispers.

When I opened them again, I watched Sam glance sidelong and smile, her dimples deepening. Hesitating only for a moment, she turned back to watch the road.

I stared at the passing green lanes. If I watched Sam, I would do something crazy like touch her. At least this way, all I could see was a blurred shadow of her in reflection.

We had to drive fifteen miles to the nearest town or about seven to the village shop, so the latter was where we went. The dusty little emporium doubled up as a post office. It was how these places were before the post office branches all closed down. Sam casually parked the van outside, jumped down and stormed around in her desert boots. I hung back.

The bell announced our arrival as we pushed the door open. The proprietor—an elderly gent—barely looked up. Sam held the shopping list of supplies, including ingredients that would fulfil Lucian's meal requests. He'd won, as always. Sam grabbed the food efficiently and I helped her load the bags in the van. I thought we were heading straight back to the camp, but she sat down on a bench in the village green outside of the shop. Her flat chest and strong muscle stretched the tank top.

She extended her long legs and waved me over. "Come on, take a break."

I sat down with a stomach full of butterflies. I wanted to be with her, but I was also afraid of betraying my attraction to her. She lit a cigarette, inhaled the smoke and blew it out slowly, savouring the taste.

"Want one?" She held out the pack. I shook my head. I couldn't help but enjoy sitting next to her, sharing the brief break, despite my apprehension.

"What was it like at college?" I asked when Sam finished her cigarette. I'd probably subconsciously wanted a safe subject.

Leaning across the back of the bench, she propped her head up with her hand and looked intently at me. "I had a good time. I belonged to all kinds of clubs. There were so many activities. So much to discover and so little time. I used to run a lesbian film club once a month."

I swallowed. My guess was correct, and now I didn't know what I'd do with that knowledge.

She sat up again, crossing her legs, and took a swig from her water bottle. As if she was reading my mind, she added, "I realised I was into girls when I was maybe eleven."

Avoiding her gaze, I focused on a stray lint in my T-shirt, pretending that the heat inside of me didn't exist.

Sam stood up abruptly as though she was startled by a revelation. "Come on. We'd better drive back."

We got in the van, and Sam pulled away from the village. I wondered how she had begun working with children with disabilities. Did she study the subject at college?

I might have asked the question aloud, or, she kept guessing what I was thinking. Uncanny.

"I went to Oxford and majored in Physics. So, nothing to do with disabilities and children."

I half turned, while trying to keep my eyes on the road. Physics sounded so clever. None of my classmates made it to Oxbridge. I'd gone to the local college for my A' levels and my acceptance by the London university was already an exceptional result.

I wanted to listen to her talk forever. "Any advice for me?"

"You're going after the summer, yeah? Well, I'd say live your life. There's so much beyond the walls of our universities, outside of book learning." She gazed out of the windshield, her right elbow resting on the open window, while she kept her left hand on the wheel. Casually, not a care in the world.

"Shouldn't you be solving mathematical problems or something? What made you work with these kids?"

She shrugged. "I wanted to do something real, to actually make a difference, have a direct impact on someone's life. Oxford was fun but it was too privileged. All my classmates' parents had villas in Europe."

I wondered if she really believed that or if she was telling me because I was clearly a local lass who was not particularly well off. The point about making an impact, too, was inspiring.

"I'm going to be the first in my family to go to university," I mused. My dad was an electrician before he had an affair and left, and my mum was a hairdresser. I was basically a working-class girl without a hint of sophistication.

Sam asked me what I was about to study and why. When I told her that I was 'interested in people', she laughed.

She tried to stop herself, causing the van to swerve. Luckily there was no traffic on these country lanes. "Sorry. It's honourable. Really. I'm sorry to be such a cynic. I don't think university equips us to face the real world, though, whether you study physics or sociology."

Later, when I too was out there 'in the real world', I thought of Sam and how she might have planted that seed in me about how to live my life, that I should make a difference. At that time, speaking with someone ten years older than me was revelatory. It was as though Sam was speaking a new language structured by the grammar of life.

As we drove on, I thought about wanting to be like her, and then immediately chided myself for sounding like a child. *What do you want to be when you grow up?* I wanted to be like Sam. I knew by instinct that I would be a different person by the end of the working holiday. It was exhilarating and frightening at the same time.

School, which broke up only some weeks before, already seemed so far away. That was the old me, and this boy Jerome had liked that me. Tall, broad, muscular and dreadlocked. He was lots of girls' wet dream. Last year, he'd asked me out to the movies one Saturday night. It was supposed to be an instant cult film that Jerome had sworn was the next big thing. We ate subs for dinner and tried to converse.

I like hip-hop.

Oh, no. Left field for me.

Football.

Hmm, swimming.

Pizza. Fried chicken.

We'd found that we had absolutely nothing in common. We chuckled.

Opposites could attract.

Yeah, you're great but I don't really think it's happening.

We'd laughed some more. He bought way too much popcorn, and the cult film was too obscure for either of us to understand. *But there's cool music in the score.* Still, it was a good first date, and we'd kissed. It was more a sweet peck than a passionate tongue twist. I wondered what the athletic Jerome was doing now.

"Did you say you're going to study sociology at uni?" Sam jolted me out of my musings.

I repeated my non-existent résumé and why I'd chosen the subject.

She nodded, as if she understood. I supposed ten years were enough to make someone realise what one should have done and what could have happened. Should. Could. Would. All the words that meant little to the youthful me. So, I did the only thing that I felt like doing and watched her from the passenger seat and smiled. She glanced back at me when she could and returned with a grin, showing off the two subtle dimples that graced the edges of her mouth. What if my feelings were entirely one-sided? It'd be embarrassing, and I'd have to live through the humiliation for the next week.

DAY 6

THE WALK TOOK in a pine forest and stream. Most of the kids came despite varying degrees of disability. Eric seemed excited alongside Tim, his hands flapping. He smiled wide, saliva dripping down his chin. Tim wiped it away.

It was only a few kilometres, but the hike was a challenge to someone like Eric and the younger ones. Lucian had no problem physically, but he didn't seem able to get his head around the following-in-a-line part. It was making my job that much harder, but I was also amused by his ability to make the walk so much more exciting. I'd learned over the last few days that unless he was drawing or writing, he found it hard to stay still.

"Lucian, where are you going?" He'd already run off to an invisible target. I wasn't sure if he could hear me, so I ran after him down a shaded side track. He knelt down and touched the thorns of some brambles, lost in a world of his own.

"Be careful of the sharp needles." I sank down to his level.

He withdrew his hands but continued to look at the varied vegetation.

"This one." Lucian pointed to some long stems of tiny leaves. "They close up when you touch them. See." He demonstrated. I remembered being fascinated by those, too, when I was young.

He picked up a small grit stone that was mostly white. "This is quartz. It's not so common in the Dark Peak. The Dark Peak has sedimentary rock."

I considered him. "Where did you read about this?"

He palmed the quartz. "On the internet. May I keep this?"

"Of course." He would go on to collect quite a few keepsakes from our trips out.

I'd have liked him to do whatever he wanted but we needed to follow the group. "Come on." I had to herd him along to keep up with the others, and borrowing a leaf from Sam's command book was as good as any.

He reluctantly stood up, and we walked side by side back to the main path. "I don't like this," he muttered. And again and again he told me how he disliked hiking. We soldiered on regardless.

Our steps were sometimes soft on the soil ground, and sometimes hard on the crunchy leaves and branches. When we were shrouded in the thicket, I used my body to open a path, disturbing the brambles, while Lucian followed. As we walked close to each other, I became more aware that he was taller and broader than me even though he was three years younger. Sometimes I'd forget his age because his facial expression was blander than his peers, so I couldn't employ the same communication tools that I'd use with other teenagers, like the younger pupils at my school. At those moments, I felt bad for treating him like a child. But I was learning fast. Every day, I discovered Lucian's quirks and understood them better.

He was challenging himself. I knew that. Trips were unpredictable, but he was forewarned and he'd forced himself to participate as much as he could. Whenever we joined in an activity, he'd stare and then followed my lead stoically. His growing trust in me had started from the fork incident.

I glanced back over my shoulder to see that he'd picked up a bit of speed. My urge was to hold his hand, but he wouldn't appreciate it.

"All right?"

He nodded.

A few minutes later. "Josie, shall we go down that path?" He pointed to another track that promised greater adventures.

I discovered on this walk that paths were star attractions to him. Lucian wanted to explore all of them. He was a walking contradiction. He liked order and couldn't stand anything unscheduled, but he was also fascinated by nature, which was unpredictable.

I saw the next pair of host and guest about six feet in front of us. "No, Lucian. We're staying on the main trail, remember? If we explore every side track, we will never reach the top."

Lucian's arms flopped to his sides but reluctantly he continued.

We'd been walking in dusk under the layer of trees, the morning light only filtering through the gaps in the woods occasionally. We'd come to an opening because I could feel the warmth of the sun on my face and exposed arms. Instead of quickening our steps, we stopped because Lucian had. He closed his eyes and tilted his head to face the sun. I stood next to him.

I wasn't going to ask what he was doing; I simply copied his gesture. When I closed my eyes and faced the rays, I saw the afterglow that was brighter than ever. The colours lingered long.

He taught me when I tried to see without my eyes, the vision was all the more vivid. I'd learned over those days that if I only focused on one sense, it would become more vivid, like that day we listened to the rain. Lucian reached out and touched my little finger, the tiniest gesture sent a thrill through me. I knew the enormity even though his touch was feathery. An earthy scent engulfed us. I was so emotional from sharing this moment that the warm sun on my skin, the fragrance of summer, our light breaths came together like a hypnotist's chant.

This was the moment when I knew I'd courted the light. In the middle of the forest, as the stream flowed closely by. When I turned, I saw Lucian gazing at me, a rare smile on his face. He was beautiful like that.

We wanted to capture that instant and never let go, but after long minutes, I grudgingly urged us on. "Come on. We have to catch up."

We came to a small rock platform overlooking the moor. Only six of the pairs had made it up, and most of them looked tired from exertion. Eric hugged Tim, who scratched his head, embarrassed by the physical contact. The teenager hopped around a bit, delighted by his own achievement.

A breeze grazed my face as I tilted my head to catch the rays, and when I opened my eyes Sam was standing next to me, replicating my gesture. Early heather carpeted the field in front of us. I wondered if she, too, had courted the light that afternoon, whether she'd opened her heart to the spell of summer.

DAY 7

"T HIS MORNING I have two hours of drawing from ten a.m."
Lucian clutched his drawing pad, pencil case and colour pencils, waiting for me by his door.

I could almost hear a 'come on'. It seemed that was all we used in order to command. Sam was too impatient. I'd tried to coax Lucian into joining in the group activities, and he wanted his way.

He read the time on his watch and his lips thinned into a line of displeasure. "O nine fifty-eight."

I smiled because he sounded like he was in the military or some other regimented environment. I guess in a way he was in his own strict regime.

We went to the day room. Some of the other kids were running around outside, using the adventure playground. Lucian had decided he'd grown too big for most of the outdoor facilities here, though I gathered he didn't feel comfortable with too many stimulants around.

We found two seats close to the window. He laid the pencils out neatly and started drawing. Yellow dots in neat rows and columns within a circle. Petals delicately graced the edge of the sphere. I read a book while letting him create. Peace and calm claimed me.

After filling the paper completely with exquisite yellow flowers, he took out a fine black pen and added thin strands.

"Sunflowers?" I asked. We'd looked at them yesterday in the grounds of the activity centre. Lucian had tilted his head and squinted in the sun and observed, and memorised. His flowers were absolutely stunning and life-like. They were shining and proudly present under the sun.

"Hmm," he answered. I was glad he'd found new subjects to draw while on this trip.

When he finished the first drawing, he carefully tore it from the pad and started immediately on the next one. A frown formed on his forehead as he concentrated.

"Lucian, what do you do with your drawings?" I imagined his room at home full of neat piles of these acutely observed pictures.

"Mum helps me put them in files."

As I thought. They'd never see the light of day but lay happily, recording his mind.

I took up the first drawing. "Do you ever give them to anyone? Or show them off? I mean, I'd love to have this as a reminder of the camp, if it's okay with you." I felt as though I was exploiting him, to even ask for his creation like this.

He looked up from the piece of paper and stared at me for a brief moment. "You mean…you think they're good?"

"Yes, absolutely. More than good. Has no one told you so?" I felt bad for him if that was the case.

Lucian shook his head slowly. "Usually, only my mum sees them really. She loves them. I have categories, and she helps me put my drawings away." He went back to his art, and didn't give the drawing to me. I didn't press.

Sam and I took the bikes out to the village store when the kids were having their afternoon nap. It was as if Sam made excuses about things we needed, because the holiday complex was well stocked. Sam's strong legs pedalling became an enduring image, while I struggled to keep up, changing gears a little too late on the undulating country paths.

"Come on!" she shouted over her shoulder as we rode the few miles out to the shop.

The hot sun had come out during those July weeks. I was soon sweating with the exertion, but it was exhilarating at the same time as the wind blew in my face.

The dusty small post office and general store was the nearest spot of civilisation to the camp. Sam stealthily brought out her packet of cigarettes. She couldn't smoke around the kids, so she'd have one when we were away from the group. She grinned like a naughty child because we were taking a breather from work, bunking off during the guests' afternoon rest. A cigarette in her mouth, she leaned against the stone cottage that housed the shop, her slender frame perfectly moulding to the mossy grey.

"Come on," she whispered when she finished the ciggie. I followed, inhaling the lingering scent of cigarette smoke as we entered the shop. A bell rang over our heads, announcing our arrival to the proprietor.

Sam took too long pouring over relic merchandise, pointing some out so we could giggle under our breaths. Pairs of flesh-coloured tights with packaging that might have dated back to the 1980s, teddy bears still in wrappers but which appeared to have seen better days. Sun-bleached pale labels. We drifted over to the food section, which fared no better.

I chuckled at the two kinds of limp white bread, tins of beans and carrots. I dreaded reading their sell-by dates.

Sam eyed the small chest freezer. "What about an ice lolly? Would you like one, Josephine?" She was working hard to suppress her glee.

I pouted. "I'm not twelve."

Opening the heavy glass door of the small freezer, she pulled out a multicoloured tube. "I want one."

I stopped her hand that was closing the cold door. "Me too." The warmth of our joined hands contrasted with the temperature of the ice stick.

She paid the owner and we walked out. Cycling several miles to the nearest store and eating ice lollies... It was the kind of extravagance that one could only indulge in during the summer holidays. We stood by the side wall of the squat building and tore open the wrappers. Between licking and biting into the ice, we grinned at each other.

All around us, as if transformed by childish magic, the mossy summer air chimed. Birds chirped overhead. The smiles on our faces never left.

I was so close to Sam, I smelled a faint scent of something lightly flowery. Jasmine, perhaps. I'd always associate that fragrance with the heady sensation of attraction to a hot-blooded woman. The tattoo on her skull fascinated me. A no-entry sign peeked out from under the short stubble. Did she know my desire for her, and would she decide to spend the next week fighting it and taunting me, ignoring whatever was hanging in the air until it was time to go home?

She leaned in and licked my lolly. Mine was lime and lemon and tangy to taste. I shook my head at her childlike behaviour. While she wasn't looking at me, I returned the favour. She had some kind of multicoloured fruit stick that tasted like berries. That earned me a laugh from her.

We clicked our lollies together as though we were toasting. To what, I wasn't sure, but as our faces neared each other, I was captured by the warmth, by an imagination of togetherness. It felt as though the world had become only the two of us, and I didn't want to have to return home. I didn't want to think about university. Perhaps stolen moments were the most precious. They were fleeting; they kept us on edge. *Is this the day when we'll take the van out for a short chat down a country lane? Will we cycle to the village and get an ice cream or lolly again?* Most days we were far too busy looking after the kids to do anything. The actions that were not repeated only became imprinted in my mind as the best representations of the summer.

In my room, I found a postcard that I'd packed with me to write home. On the small rectangle, I drew the cartoon of a girl eating an ice lolly. She had short hair and freckles, as the sun bore down on her. It made me think of Lucian's drawings, though, which were so controlled and detailed. I couldn't draw like that. Mine was free and childlike. I never sent the postcard home.

Later, Tim had gone out with a couple of the other workers. Their mission was to find the nearest pub and have a drink. I could understand it. Some of the volunteers were leaving tomorrow and their replacements would arrive. The constant demands of our guests were driving some of us insane. Caring for Lucian was hard work and exhausting, but I was glad that he didn't have to get used to another helper. I was learning new things every day. I sensed Lucian's trust in me developing, manifested in small things like his furtive glances at me. Minor victories felt like triumphs.

But tonight, I'd stayed behind, craving solitude. I liked Tim and I got on with all the other volunteers, but it was also a rare opportunity to be silent. I went to see the willow tree that I'd discovered next to a stream, and walked a few miles on my own, meeting no one on the way.

Then I read in bed and wrote in my journal. The moon was bright enough to cast light into the room while I worked under the desk lamp. I'd written about Sam, and put the diary carefully in the locker in case anyone should read about my infatuation. My eyes drooped eventually but I couldn't get to sleep.

The night chill had little effect on my imagined heat. I changed the sheet, so it was crisp and fresh against my bare skin. I lifted my vest but the cool surface of the cotton couldn't calm the emotions that surged through me. I took the vest off and tossed it to the wall side. I needed to be discreet in case Tim came back early. My knickers were next to be shed. I hid my hands under the cover and they found my naked body. My breast met the bed sheet and the pillow pressed to my cheek as a substitute caress. Soon, my rubbing hands were not enough.

A faceless body pushing into me. I sought more friction. Gradually my senses heightened when I could in my mind's eye see the body that defined pleasure. I gasped but I still suppressed any noises I was issuing. She had gentle curves and hard lines. Beautiful amber eyes and firm muscles pressed against me. I gripped her head, threading my fingertips through the short stubble, and clenched my jaw as the two contrasting shades of our bodies collided. I thrust harder and harder until white spots like melting snow appeared in front of my eyes.

Her image crystallised, seeped into my consciousness, my dreams, and my world turned upside down.

DAY 8

OVER THE FIRST week, we'd settled into a routine, which was great for Lucian's sensibility. He still stared at his timetable every day and frowned if there was a slight variation. I hated to break it to him, but Sam was a pragmatist, which meant Lucian might have to force himself to be just that little bit flexible. Otherwise, I let him win the small battles.

"Would you like some orange juice?" I filled a jug for our lunch.

"Would you like some orange juice?" Lucian stared at the glass with his big eyes.

All of a sudden, I saw through the clear blue. There was so much intelligence inside of him, bursting to be let out, but it wasn't something most people could understand. He had a differently brilliant mind that we 'real people' couldn't fathom.

"Quit it!" I bounced back. "Just drink the juice. Don't you play up your disability just to make me cross." I smiled to show that I was joking and poured him a small glass of orange juice.

Lucian sipped from his glass and grimaced. He confronted me again. "Oh, you are angry. You'll have to consult your instructions. How to deal with an autistic child one-o-one." He picked up his sandwich—ham and cheese, no extras—and took a bite.

I feigned annoyance. "Ha-ha. Very funny. Just finish your lunch."

"Good job I'm eating a sandwich. We won't have another fork incident, will we?"

I narrowed my eyes at his cheek, but I secretly enjoyed the teasing. "I think I much prefer the rigid Lucian. I thought I'd never get a laugh from you."

"I am still special needs Lucian." He bit into the sandwich with glee.

I hated that he was teased. "Don't call yourself that."

"Just special Lucian, then." He finished the juice and made another face.

I'd grown to see him that way too. "That's better."

His hand flapped once, as if it was betraying how Lucian was pleased with the nickname. He looked away.

The one pastime I had during the camp was completely Sam related. Spotting her whenever I went into group activities was fun. She would have stood out, of course, even if she was not the tallest. The two male volunteers were at least her height. In turn, I wanted her to pay attention to me while I worried that I was being too obvious to the other volunteers. I'd found out that I was the youngest of the helpers, and they would more than likely think I was being an easily impressionable kid.

I needed to find myself a nook in the extensive grounds of the camp to have a breather, to think about my newfound infatuation. The massive weeping willow tree by the stream became my sanctuary. I took breaks under it whenever I could, seeking shelter among its long hairy branches and imagining no one could see me. Inhaling the grassy scent and seeking respite from the summer heat, I'd close my eyes and have imaginary conversations with my friendly listener.

I'm sure she's interested in me.

If you say so.

She watched me yesterday when I helped Lucian with the navigation activity.

He gave me an eye-roll. She's supposed to look after everyone. Why wouldn't she be checking up on you?

Great. What should I do now? I've no one to talk to about this.

He laughed. I'd hear him.

What do you want to do?

The internal dialogue was cruel and it never went anywhere. I always took hold of the swaying willow and rested a branch against my cheek to feel the softness, as though I was holding her warm face against mine.

Do you think she has a girlfriend? What does she look like having sex?

How I blushed when I asked my willow friend, who chuckled some more because of my idiocy. Just ask her.

Thanks. What was the point of speaking to him if he only told me what I already knew?

Apart from our secret trips out to the village, nighttime presented opportunities for us to get to know each other. The British summer would last until ten at night. The volunteers usually gathered after the guests had gone to bed. Rose or Beth would make us hot chocolate or coffee.

I took my cup of cocoa to find Tim, who was speaking to Sam. Feeling nervous, I forced myself to sit down on the bench, next to Tim and facing Sam, and tried to appear as natural as possible.

The two of them were already deep in conversation. Sam waved her arms about.

"I'm vegan." She frowned. "Killing animals is unnecessary and unethical."

Tim countered, "Okay. But you don't actually kill chickens to collect their eggs. You use milk to make cheese."

"Battery hens. Dairy cows. Farm practices are dreadful, so you may as well be killing the animals." She touched her almost bald head, ran her big hand down it. The hair was growing back a little after a week.

I quietly observed the argument. As Sam was talking, she waved her hands and the smooth tan skin stretched beautifully in the setting sun. She had this small furrow on her forehead when she made a particularly important point. She'd then hang back a little to hear what Tim said in reply. Watching her like that made me want to grab her and put my lips against her cheek or perhaps the plump lips.

Tim proffered some more facts about free-range farming.

"Oh, come on! So you're going to fatten the chicken and be very nice to lucky lickin' only to slaughter it later when you feel like a bit of free-range breast meat. That's bullshit and you know it."

Come on. There were so many possible meanings to the phrase: keep up, no time to waste, discover something new.

She may consider the recipient of the imperative foolish. Or, it could be a sexual remark. *Coming on to you.*

Tim put a piece of chicken sandwich, his nighttime snack, into his mouth.

"I'm not going to bother explaining anymore," she concluded with a sulk.

I loved her conviction, and I bought what she was arguing easily. I was silently following, discovering, finding myself ignorant. Conscious or not, her bold remarks made me notice her more. I was stunned by my wanting a girl for her sex for the first time. How her breast protruded proudly. What her nipples might taste like and how she might react to my tongue running down her arm.

Sam was persuasive, and now I felt guilty at the thought of dead meat in my mouth. I stared at my cup of hot drink. "I think I'll try being a vegetarian, too."

Sam beamed at me. Tim's eyes went from me to her face but he didn't comment.

The weather changed again, and it was torrid for three days as though it reflected my mood. I lay there at night remembering her flushed face when she was excited. Tim snored faintly, rhythmically. My hand meandered down my body. I turned and hid under the thin cover, face down. Suppressing any sounds I might make, I lifted my T-shirt and rubbed myself against the soft pad underneath. My mind drifted to her, to the silky skin and strong bony limbs. I wrapped myself around her.

No, the light was not broken, but in the darkness it had a different kind of radiance. If I seek it, I'll find it.

Life at the summer camp was intense. During the day, we didn't have time to think about much else. Minor crises were always around the corner. I knew my time there was running out, but I'd pushed it to the back of my mind, to block out the 'real life' that I'd soon return to. I couldn't envisage what it was before this, before knowing Lucian and Sam. All the days took on a vibrancy that couldn't be possible. In my mind, it was given an importance that even the three years at university wouldn't rival.

In years to come, my memory of those hazy days morphed into imagined scenes where I'd spent time in her room and we'd talked and laughed and she'd touched me. My memory told me it was all true or at least that those scenes were based on some kind of experience.

When I told my girlfriend, she laughed and pretended to be jealous. Because Sam *had* asked for me, and we'd kissed in the tiny box room that served as her temporary domicile, she made every other bed I'd sleep in take on less significance, and all other arms and legs I'd touch intimately different from hers insofar as they had come *after*.

After that year.

DAY 9

Y OU LOOK AT her all the time."

"Who?" I knew who Lucian was referring to, but I thought I'd get away with pleading ignorance. The thing was, Lucian was observant. He remembered everything and was direct about it all.

"The leader."

Lucian didn't do eye-rolling, but I could see it. He was mocking me, and I enjoyed his sense of humour. So unexpected and hidden, as though I was only allowed in through a secret door that opened infrequently.

"You make this sound like one of your futuristic dystopian sci-fis." It was his preferred genre, and he'd read the same book again and again. All his books were dog-eared and well-used. Philip K. Dick. Huxley. *The Time Machine*. Classic science fiction in paperback. I wondered what he made of it. The perpetual allegory of our present day, just like the summer camp being a concentrated form of socialisation for me, and we were controlled and manipulated by the great leader. The invisible eyes were everywhere, affecting us, as if this was a panopticon.

I wondered if there was some truth in Lucian's vision. Maybe we were only constrained by the limits of our own imagination. Were we all trapped by superimposed norms and unable to break out? He was the one who was looking at that conventional world and laughing at the 'real people'.

He stared at the table next to me for long moments. He wasn't smiling but there was a rare inflection of his lips. "I saw you and her, and the way you always follow her with your eyes. You two are like these people on television. My mum said they're love stories."

Oh, gosh. "What do they do on telly?" I shouldn't have asked one of the kids, but strangely, I felt at ease with Lucian who oscillated between childhood innocence and an all-seeing sage.

"They fall in love and stuff." *They.* I stopped for a second. Lucian knew. The one person who people probably did not expect to comprehend emotions understood my attraction to Sam perfectly. And he hadn't shown any strong reaction. He was as matter-of-fact about it as he was about how he wanted his boiled egg in the morning.

Fall in love. I blinked several times and felt wetness around my eyes.

Lucian carried on drawing his grassy field picture while talking to me. He didn't see the tears fighting to surge. Perhaps he was the last person I should be speaking to about this. About how a woman with a shaved head and a tattoo on her skull was drawing my attention.

I pretended to look at his pictures. After the lights that he kept drawing last week, we'd seen so much more this week: the moors, heather, forest leaves. Trip after trip had expanded all our horizons. The last few days, he'd been doing these intricate drawings of grass with minuscule green stems as well as the sunflowers.

"Well, what are you going to do?" He carefully put back his green pencil.

"What do you mean?" I frowned because I wasn't expecting Lucian to be interested in my personal life. But I was confused as to what he had asked me.

"About the leader." He brought a pen out of his case and added black lines on the picture. It was as if the strands of grass had come alive and they were swaying in the wind.

I gazed at his face and thought about what he might experience as love. As if he heard my thoughts, he shrugged. "Yeah, I've thought about the people on telly. I've used my right hand."

Ouch. Too much information. I coughed. But Sam said something about not being able to get social cues, though. "You're not supposed to notice these things."

"I can see the way you look at each other." He'd taught me the restriction of those assumptions. Of course, Lucian would know about love and probably crave it as much as any other boy.

"I'm sorry to assume you don't think about love."

His head remained inclined towards the drawing. Detailed strands of grass punctuated by black streaks now, separating light from dark. The blank among the colours accentuated the brightness.

"Why are you sorry? You don't know what I think about." His face was almost buried in the drawing; his hands delicately danced across the sheet of cartridge paper.

"So, what do you suggest I should do about the leader?" I found myself asking Lucian for advice. Chuckles threatened to bubble up my throat due to the irony.

Lucian stared at the spot next to my face. "I guess you can try telling her." He'd put it in such a starkly plain way, as if my willow friend had come alive.

It's simple, really.

The campfire nights were the highlights of the week. We could roast marshmallow and nuts, sit around and sing songs. The children adored it, especially the melted gluey sweets. Sam played the guitar. She had a good voice and was not afraid to launch into a song whenever it took her fancy. She was usually joined by some of the volunteers and the kids.

But the fire scared Lucian, so this was the first time he'd come out.

"Oh no. No." Lucian backed away.

"It's okay." I asked, "May I hold your hand? We can walk closer. I promise you won't burn."

Lucian stood there, his gaze fixed on the scene, considering the possibility. He held his hand out tentatively and I took it. He half wanted to try and half wanted to escape back to his room.

It wouldn't matter if he didn't join in, but I wished he could experience the campfire, something that he was unlikely to have at home.

Linking hands, we approached slowly, advancing a few inches at a time. At some point, his fingers tightened around mine. I squeezed his hand as a reassurance.

We sat five feet away where the fire didn't reach but we'd still see the glow of the flames on the others' faces and hear the songs. That was good enough for me. Lucian faced the side but the orange and yellow lit his cheeks up. He covered his ears for a while. I brought him some syrupy nuts and a hot chocolate, which he took. His hands didn't go back to protecting him afterwards.

I waited impatiently until the others had drifted to bed one by one. Lucian wanted to go and read by nine o'clock, so I took him back to his bedroom. When Tim eventually bid his good night, I was elated and uncomfortable at the same time. Sam and I were alone. I stared at the flames until my eyes hurt, but I refrained from looking at her. I understood the benefits of avoiding eye contact now. My rational self told me to return to my room and get out while I was still head above water.

She was strumming a song that I didn't recognise. Her voice wasn't traditionally trained, but it had a certain appeal—sultry, honeyed and, at this time of the night, alluring.

When Sam glanced up from playing, she caught me looking at her. So intensely. Warmth rose in my face but I hoped she wouldn't realise what it was and would put it down to the red heat from the campfire.

The light flickered over Sam's skin. Rouge. Orange. Glow. Blue streaks appeared among the flames every so often. I gave in to my urge to touch her exposed arm, tracing the light that danced on her warm flesh, and she let me. It had to be the worst cliché to imagine myself the moth flying towards the light, but the image consumed me and I couldn't turn away. My hands were clammy and I couldn't decide where to put them. I felt ridiculous all of a sudden but couldn't stop myself.

We sat so close that our knees touched.

She stopped strumming. I saw her swallow with the vague ripple of her throat. After long moments, Sam put the guitar down gently on the floor and stood. She ran back to the house and brought out two opened bottles of beer. I wasn't used to drinking and was already a little light-headed. She took a generous gulp, so I followed. I felt drunk and dizzy. When I was eighteen, I'd be tipsy after a couple of beers. I was a complete lightweight.

After swallowing a mouthful of lager, I burped.

"You're drunk!" Sam sounded amused.

I hiccupped as well, proving that she was absolutely right. Then I laughed alongside her. "I don't drink much."

"You'll have plenty of opportunities when you get to uni." She squinted at the flames that were flickering in her eyes. "The first proper drinking session I had when I was a freshman, I puked a mixture of cider and vodka. It was disgusting. I did it right at the feet of the Jacqueline du Pré statue."

"Who's Jack… Dupré?"

Sam laughed some more. "Jacqueline. I think she was a famous cellist. The music department at St Hilda—my college— was named after her. Anyway, I've not touched cider since."

She picked up the guitar again, and started to pluck the strings and hum a song. I didn't know what the song was called then, but it'd made an impression on me. So, I found it afterwards. *Perfect. It's got to be perfect.* I wondered if she'd sung it because she'd considered those moments perfect or she was lamenting about relationships in general. Perhaps she was in a perfect love affair. Or, she was warning me that I should wait for the perfect person. There was no telling.

We are forever double guessing when it comes to matters of the heart. When we are young, we may believe in perfection, but we won't know how to find it or cherish it even if there is such a thing. When we get older, after too many failures, we regret not waiting for our soul mates and no longer believe in happily-ever-afters.

In front of the campfire, I thought I was as close to perfection as possible.

The fire was crackling now while the red, yellow and orange mingled, struggling to give out more warmth. We'd waited until we could be alone, as if we had a secret pact to spend some stolen moments together. We were both overstaying, willing each other to want company.

I had been staring at her ear stud long enough. I reached out and touched it. "What does the black triangle mean?"

Sam's face turned serious for a second. "The Nazis persecuted gays and lesbians, as well as Jews. They made them wear emblems: yellow stars for Jews, pink triangles for gays and black triangles for lesbians. Well, we believe they did. It was for the asocial or *arbeitsscheu*—work-shy."

I was stunned. I learned history at school, but I hadn't a clue that they imprisoned and killed more than Jews. I thought of Jason, my gay school friend, but Sam was the first lesbian I'd met properly. Wearing the black triangle on her small shapely ear was a kind of interpellation. *Come on, I'm a dyke and I'm proud of it.* I'd never even thought that anyone should hide their sexuality but it made sense. It was defiance.

Years later I'd start doing the same: joining the Pride parade and waving the rainbow flag. At that age, I was too sheltered to know. I was bright and I'd got into a good secondary school where the few working class kids like me were the exceptions. Even so, I lacked experience or friends who were different. It made sense why I was naturally drawn to Jason.

I came back from my reflections to meet her curious eyes, light dancing in her pale-brown irises. Her face coloured golden.

"I like you like this." I couldn't work out where that came from. Speaking my thoughts was dangerous. It left me wide open but I was too drunk to think straight. I wasn't exactly socially awkward, nothing compared to what Lucian had to deal with in any case, but I was mostly quiet and reserved. I usually waited until everyone else had had a say before I piped up. That's just the way I was.

Sam smiled, the tenderness incompatible with the tough façade. She ruffled my short fluffy hair with one hand. *I like you too.* I licked my lips but refused to accept that a kiss could be negotiated. Instead, I closed my eyes, but the bright fire was already imprinted in my mind and it refused to leave.

The afterglow made me think of Lucian's drawings. "There are sixteen lights arranged in rows of eight and two columns."

She laughed. "Now you sound like Lucian."

"Yeah." Because he saw light in a beautiful way, courting it, caressing it. I didn't realise my fingertips skated across her arm up to her long neck.

She caught my hand and our linked digits were electric, as if the fire was nearer and stronger than it actually was. When she caressed the back of my hand, I gazed at the outdoor light back at the centre that was shedding an orange glow over us. A couple of moths raced towards the brightness, flapping their wings to their destiny, just like the vision I'd had earlier. I wondered if we were all animals like that, unable to control our own emotions and wanting so desperately to reach the glow in our hearts only to realise that we'd get burned and die a little in the process.

"Can I come to you tonight?"

"No, not tonight, or any night." Sam's lips thinned but her eyes sparkled. The deep amber drew me in. "You're not so much older than Lucian and Eric. I work with teenagers."

"But they let me come as a volunteer." I reasoned, "Isn't it arbitrary that they're considered disabled and need looking after, and I'm not? There must be something I'm terrible at, like I find the violin impossible to learn. Am I musically disabled?"

I smiled. I was pretty good with languages but completely lousy with sciences at school, too.

Sam returned the grin but she shook her head. "It's society's expectation that we should all be independent. Can Eric ever live by himself? Sadly, it's unlikely. Lucian, I don't know. He seems to function quite well. So, he can probably learn one day."

"Do you know much about Lucian?"

Sam shook her head. "Probably no more than you. Last year, I had a brief conversation with his mum at the end of the holiday. She was ever so grateful for the respite care. His dad left them claiming he couldn't cope with Lucian's disability. She said he was having affairs while she struggled to care for her son and was mostly housebound."

"Bastard." *Does Lucian know all that?*

Sam nodded in agreement. Her hand on mine stopped stroking. As though she needed to disconnect from me, she removed her hand. She fumbled in her pocket, drew out a cigarette, and lit it. Her gaze was drawn back to mine, though.

She sucked on her cigarette as smoke snaked up and obscured her face. After long moments, when I thought she wouldn't say anything, she uttered, "You don't lose that pure heart now."

And you could have my heart. I hated myself for wanting to get her attention that way, and braced for disappointment.

"Are you…" I hesitated. "…interested in my heart?" There, I'd confessed, and what she did with it was no longer my responsibility.

For a long moment, I thought she wasn't going to reply. She blew more smoke clouds towards the sky. After an age, and after I'd given up knowing the answer, she casually drawled, "I have this theory. If something won't be remembered after a few months, no matter how important it seems today, it's still a frivolity."

A frivolity. I wondered. Was it me, my heart or her own sanity?

Sam sighed. "You and I. We belong to that category."

I think that day, shrouded in the hazy glow of the fire that was dimming, Sam believed that. She thought I'd forget about her after the camp, like soap bubbles that were destined to evaporate. But it did mean she thought there was a 'you and I'. And if so, wasn't that important even if it was short-lived?

"I can never do anything I'd like to do with you, y'know?" Sam stubbed out the cigarette end, rubbing her trainer over it a little too forcefully.

"Why not?" She was damn clever to throw me too many balls to juggle at once. The more pertinent question here was what she'd like to do with me, but I was too distracted by her refusal.

Her face flushed, but she wasn't going to elaborate.

"You really think it's because I'm too young?" I hated how I sounded; maybe I was proving that was exactly the case.

A few days ago, I didn't even know I was into girls. And now, I was propositioning the most enigmatic woman I'd met and bracing myself for rejection. Would it matter indeed? Would I remember this in a few months, in years to come? I gazed at Sam's face intently. I couldn't tell her how shocked I was by wanting her, by finding myself needing her. And yet, it all made sense. How I'd felt like an alien in a straight world, and hadn't realised that was the case until then.

I thought about how my family might respond. I hardly saw my dad after he'd left and set up home with a younger woman. My older brother always thought I did and said things just to be different. I bet he would declare that this was the beginning of a phase. *Just a phase.* Did I wish it was only that? Would it have made things easier for me? I had no hindsight that summer. Everything was forward. Going in one direction, towards the light.

My parents and brother didn't have to live my life. I did.

Sam's sigh was almost inaudible. "You should never look down on yourself because of your youth. I'd have liked to be in your place."

"But you did imply I was too young for you."

Her warm palm moved to the small of my back, and it stayed there, with all the excitement and expectation that it brought. I'd understand later that as we age, we lose a lot along the way. People say we gain wisdom or something similar, but it never replaces what we've left behind. It's not a balance sheet.

The city, the heather, that perpetual warm sunshine in July were once experienced and then reappeared only in my dreams.

My home town would feel different after all this, too, as though the city was even more vibrant. I'd spend much of my youth roaming the canal-side bars and the rundown area with its warehouses and curry cafes whenever I was home. And I have tried to cling onto all of that.

She patted my neck a couple of times, affectionately, and then she stood up. "Time for bed, I think. The kids get up too fucking early. Come on."

She lent me her hand, this time just to pull me up.

DAY 10

SAM ASKED ME to help her with the shopping in town. We were quiet on the drive there and in the store. She followed her shopping list efficiently and I helped. We were avoiding the awkward day-after conversation. And yet everything was still up in the air. Nothing resolved. Too many possibilities.

On the way back, she put on a local radio station. The passing sunlight through the slightly smeared window nearly lured me to an afternoon nap, but I recognised the detour. On an unfamiliar country path a few miles away from our activity centre, Sam stopped the van. A bend created a serendipitous parking space. She reversed the van with its back to the yellow field in front of it.

"Come on, a little rest?" She winked.

I was still staring at the clear blue sky when Sam hopped down from the van with boundless energy. She opened the boot up and laid out a couple of blankets in the hollow space, adding our backpacks as pillows. I was amused by what she was planning.

She lay down and patted the space next to her. "What do you think of this?" She gestured to the field and the sky, a horizon that seemed to stretch for miles.

I shook my head but joined her anyway, lying flat with my back on the blanket. It was a perfect position under the opened boot to watch the clouds flying by like white cotton. From that perspective, it was only the blue sky and our trainers floating in the air. Instead of gazing at the sun, I shifted my scrutiny to the two pairs of legs stretched out pointing to the horizon. Sam wore dark-coloured chinos. Mine were washed jeans. Our pumps in white, blue and yellow against the backdrop of the summer clouds. It was picture perfect: her dark, heavy trousers and my ripped jeans against the fields of yellow grass. We didn't speak for a long time. The idyllic scene, the colours, Sam's closeness, her golden skin would become forever etched in my memory as the summer's riches.

My willow friend was right. I wanted to ask her so many things and I should, but I didn't. I tacitly understood that it would have been a hopeless pursuit. I was off to London. She was ten years older, I guessed, and working in the North of England. We hardly exchanged much personal information. What people might ask if they were interested in each other. *How old are you? Where do you live? What's your favourite food? Would you like to go out on a date?* I wanted to keep her in a little box in my imagination, cocooned and preserved for that summer only. I didn't want to care that she had a life outside of this, whatever this was.

I loved the residual light that I'd see after staring at a bright spot for too long. *Chiaroscuro.* Light and shadow play off each other and become one.

Sam moved her leg so the toe of her left foot touched my right, our chores long forgotten. This was a hell of a detour.

We conversed intermittently about the camp.

"I don't think I'm any better than these people who look down on the disabled. At first, I was so frightened by Eric and even Lucian. I mean, he doesn't look different, but…" I admitted.

Sam turned her oval face to my side. The more I watched her, the more I realised how very symmetrical her features were.

"It's okay to be imperfect. For me, imperfection may be about doing my job badly or getting frustrated or impatient with the kids. For someone like Lucian, I don't know. He doesn't care for things that people assume we should have."

"Like what?"

Sam touched her head. "I don't know. For a teenager, maybe he should care about being popular, winning sports competitions, a first girlfriend."

"Maybe he wants those things." I thought about his drawings, his books, and the way he flapped about and couldn't concentrate except when he was drawing or reading.

"Yeah, probably." Sam sat up a little and grabbed her water bottle for a sip. "My brother Matt has Asperger's."

I also propped myself up on my elbow so I was facing her. "Is that why you've chosen to work with disabled kids?"

"I suppose. Partly. Growing up with Matt and living with his condition make me see having a disability as the norm, y'know."

I could imagine. "What's your brother like?"

"I think Matt has all the classic Asperger difficulties. He's socially awkward, can't make friends easily because he doesn't know how to empathise with others. Clumsy. Matt breaks things all the time. Direct. He was home-schooled as well." Sam inhaled. "But you know what? He has the most brilliant mind, almost like a cliché. He taught himself Japanese in three months."

How I wished I had that kind of linguistic ability. "Did he go to university?"

Sam nodded. "Matt tried for a while. He was there for a year and a half but doing the coursework and exams was too much. He just wasn't wired that way. He dropped out and went travelling. My parents were so worried about him."

"But, was he okay?"

Sam nodded. She fished a cigarette out of her bag and lit it. "Yeah, he didn't tell us much about what he'd done, but he travelled through China and Japan and learned the languages quickly. He's amazing."

I gazed at her profile, loving how her long lashes left a shadow on her cheeks. I wanted to reach out, to touch the smooth skin. But instead, I continued my enquiries in a bid to understand autism. "What does he do now?"

"Hmm. Not much. He helps my dad out with his company. It's a kind of part-time job." She shrugged and took a long drag of her cigarette.

"Lucian's just differently wired, or something like that," I mused. "I find him fascinating."

Sam smiled. "That's what I think of my brother. He's not 'disabled' so much as simply neuro-atypical. Does it make sense?"

"That's the right way to describe it. It feels like Lucian sees and interprets the world in a different way. His drawings are absolutely stunning."

She watched me for a second and took my hand into hers. I stared at our joined hands and wondered what I should do about it.

"You're doing a great job with him. It's hard to be with someone in such an intense way." *And thinking about intimacy when you know so little about someone.*

I managed to respond. "I've been really enjoying the camp even though it can be difficult at times."

From day one, I'd been dying to ask her about her tattoo: the symbol for stop. A slanted line in a circle. I touched it, and the short stubble pricked my fingertip, arousing my fascination.

Sam laughed, sounding like bells. "It says: No one should brainwash me. *Ich denke Ich bin.* All thoughts are my own. I possess my own mind. Josie, you will too. Don't let the buggers tell you what to think. Even at uni. Especially at uni." Her lips thinned into a serious long dash. A sudden determination to be this independent spirit flooded my brain.

"Do you think Lucian possesses his thoughts?"

She sighed. "Of course I do. I think it's criminal that people like Lucian are considered incapable."

I nodded in agreement.

The perfect British summer was often only a few days a year, but in that remote field we had it. Light breeze blew the thick mountain of clouds along. I felt like sleeping, imagining sheep jumping over the white fluffy cumulus.

Before I did fall asleep, she squeezed my hand once more, then released it.

"Come on. We need to head back before the kids run riot and Grant gets in a flap."

Sam stood. I looked up and beamed at her. The sun was behind her, so she appeared like a mirage. A silhouette. Black against yellow. Another icon of that summer.

DAY 11

Tᴵᴹ ᴛᴏʟᴅ ᴍᴇ it was a yearly tradition when the lights in the hall were dimmed, and all the chairs were pushed back. It reminded me of school disco.

The dance hits piped out of the not-so-great music system, as Lucian had already pointed out. I was standing near the entrance waiting for him to show up, when Sam came out of nowhere and stood next to me. She refused to look at my face, though. We observed the kids, instead.

"Where did you get this muzak from?" I grinned and leaned in so she'd hear me. "It's so last year."

Sam's face-splitting laugh echoed in my head. "Look around. The kids are loving it."

The lighting wasn't like a standard club since the strobe effects were inappropriate, but there were soft-coloured lights and bubbles from a machine, and some of the kids and carers were dancing alone or with each other and smiling. Most of them were wriggling along to the ghetto blaster, currently hooked up to the loudspeakers. Even the two guests in wheelchairs manoeuvred the chairs around a bit trying to keep up with the rhythm. Their carers came along and helped them. Eric and Tim were gyrating to Abba's 'Dancing Queen', cancelling out any tics and unwanted gestures that Eric normally displayed.

My eyes shifted to search for Lucian and I saw him hovering by the far wall away from the reach of sounds and colours. I hadn't noticed him arriving. The noisy crowd would have been too much for him, but at least he was here.

I shouted into Sam's ear, "I'm going to talk to Lucian for a minute. Okay?"

She nodded and smiled, flashing her small dimples.

When I reached Lucian's side, he had his eyes closed. He looked as though he was in pain. His hands were balled into fists as if he was trying to stop them from moving.

"Hey." I had to talk quite loud for him to hear me but I was also afraid to startle him because he was standing in a way that told me he was trying to shut himself off from the rest of the room. He clearly found the noise and a hall full of dancing kids too much.

"Do you want to go back to your room?"

His eyes snapped open to reveal something unknown from a faraway place, and yet he seemed all seeing in that confined mental space. Slowly, he uttered, "I can stay. I want to try."

I nodded in agreement, grateful for his bravery. "Come on," I urged, "let us dance."

Lucian's lips lilted from his effort to smile. "I don't dance."

"Let's go through to the middle a little bit. You can keep your eyes closed and stand still. You don't have to dance. We can just listen to the music. Can I hold your hand?"

He held it out to reach for mine. His palm was clammy from worry. We headed towards the centre but kept a distance and stayed outside the edge of the main group. It wasn't the kind of music I liked dancing to either but I tried to gyrate to it. Lucian closed his eyes, as I'd suggested. I watched him as he started to subtly sway to the music. Over his shoulder I could see Sam's gaze and her faint grin. We let the moment sink in. The camp had been a place where the challenges of the outside world could not penetrate. It seemed that Lucian felt safe enough to participate.

Rebecca, a girl with Down's syndrome, walked up to Lucian and tapped on his arm. Lucian opened his eyes and squinted even though the lights were not so bright. She asked if he would like to dance with her, and he nodded; his head and right hand jerked. I created space for them and returned to the side.

I watched Rebecca and Lucian face each other and move to the sounds of nineties pop. She pasted a wide grin on her face and hopped wildly. Lucian, not looking at Rebecca directly, held his arms and fists up as if getting ready for a boxing match, but then he shifted his body, trying to keep up with his dancing companion. I smiled, wondering if he would have done this ten days ago.

I stayed as the kids started to drift off to bed. Sam had been watching the dancers with an amused smile as she leaned against the wall with arms across her front. My eyes were on her, though I tried to be as discreet as I could. Our gaze met infrequently.

Even so, her appearance next to me startled me.

"Wanna get out of here? It's not a chat-up line." I'd been the victim of her audaciousness all through the camp. How could I resist her non-chat-up?

Impulsively, I decided to take her to the stream, so my willow friend could meet her in person. After all, with three more days to go, I needed to make the most of my time with my imaginary friend.

The night walk was peaceful. The only sounds we heard were little animals and the light breeze.

"This is my spot." I waved my hand as if to introduce her to my den. The willow flowed softly. I'd come here a few times after the kids' bedtime and rested until it was time for sleep. I could stay out until nearly ten at night, taking advantage of the long summer day. After that, I'd have to use my torch.

Sam swirled three hundred and sixty degrees. She stopped and held my gaze. "Hmm. You've found an oasis." She took my hand. I closed my eyes so I could focus on the sensation of her palm.

I felt intoxicated. It was too late to worry, so I reached over and touched my lips to hers. When she didn't resist, I advanced. More, needing the return of the wet tongue.

She tasted of berries and vanilla, more feminine than her looks. The soft and lush lips pressed onto mine. I was inexperienced, though I'd kissed a boy before. I should've been thinking *am I doing this right?* But I couldn't. I needed to give the kiss all my heart and hope for the best.

My hand sought her out, resting on her neck that felt silken. How could anyone not understand the power of the connection? When two people breathe into each other seeking out what has become vital to their existence, it's no longer a simple kiss. But we always have to come apart to take a breath of air, as though we are swimming. Raise the face out of the water and catch a breath. Otherwise we drown.

Long lashes fell over her flushed cheeks. She took my breath away. Sam gasped like she needed more air.

"I won't forget this." She pulled me closer.

I thought the willow was swaying with his approval.

DAY 12

THE COMMOTION HAD escalated quickly. I ran down the corridor, through the throng of volunteers and some of the children to the wailing of Lucian that sounded like a keening animal. I found Tim among the crowd and stood next to him, paralysed as to what I could do to help.

Lucian shook his head and shouted but he wasn't making sense. He'd become a cornered creature, his territory violated by those differently reared. I could see the red rim of his eyes and the waves of his arms. The sounds he was making in between screams cut through the air like a siren.

"Damn. What happened?" I turned to Tim.

He sighed. "I think Charlotte might have used his colouring pencils without asking him. It was something small for sure."

It's not trivial. I'd been warned of this. Lucian's meltdown. Deep down, I'd been expecting and waiting for another.

A cacophony of noises was enough to unsettle anyone and certainly not helping to calm Lucian any. The kids were shouting back, all having an opinion about what had happened. The helpers offered to do *something.* Lucian had his ears covered now.

I gazed at him again; he was shaking with rage. I felt his pain. His pale cheeks were a shade of pink from the frustration and anger. He held onto his case of colour pencils tightly. It might have been a small thing for Charlotte or another kid, but it'd affected him deeply. He couldn't cope with something like that. Those pens and the personal boundary were important to him.

Sam was talking to Lucian to try to calm him down. She looked harassed since she couldn't physically constrain him. It was the first time I'd seen her appear out of control.

Lucian howled. He raised his arms over his head once more, and when he jumped with two feet and landed on the floor, the thud was strong enough to sound like a wild beast had fallen among us. He threw the case down and it fell open, the pencils scattering on the floor.

When he shakily stood back up, he grabbed his stomach with both hands as though he was in agony.

"Could we please clear the area? Now." Sam regained her composure at some point, as the kids and volunteers started to leave the corridor, going back to the day room or the bunks. At least Lucian wouldn't feel overwhelmed. I didn't leave. Couldn't.

"Sam, let me. Let me try." I stepped up next to her.

She half-turned and nodded. "You're the one he trusts."

"Lucian, buddy. Could you close your eyes for a minute for me?" I pleaded, "Please."

He looked away, unconvinced. At least he was distracted from his outburst. He momentarily stopped screaming and moving, but continued to breathe heavily, his chest heaving. Slowly, he did what I'd asked.

"How many lights? How many are there in this corridor?" I found myself closing my eyes too and trying to imagine the space.

Lucian breathed out. "Six rooms on each side. Lights between two rooms. Five on the left. Five on the right. Ten all together."

I didn't open my eyes but I could see them.

"What is the colour on the wall called?" We had looked at the colour wheel and he told me he'd memorised the numbers.

"Y11. Approximately."

After moments, I instructed him, "Now, open your eyes slowly, and breathe."

Spit had gathered at the corner of Lucian's mouth. He was still shaking with rage, with uncontrollable emotions. But he heaved and breathed out shallowly. Sam and I waited. We could see Lucian was trying hard to control himself. After minutes, he was calm enough to chance a look at me. I nodded, encouraging him.

I knelt and picked up the pencils and put them in the case, but I knew Lucian wouldn't like the disorder.

"Come on. Shall we go back to your room, Lucian?" Sam asked.

Sam and I led him back into his room. His sharers were still outside. I pulled two chairs out for him and me to sit. Sam stood against the door frame.

Lucian sat rigidly. His hands in between his thighs.

"It's okay," I whispered. He'd managed to soothe himself. I'd come to accept that meltdowns were part of him.

He slurred. "Not."

I wasn't going to argue, but instead a distraction was in order. "It's movie night. Would you like to join the others? Lucian?"

He glared at me. "No. Forty-five hours. I'll be home."

I wished he hadn't felt so bad that he was counting down the hours to go home. I wished we were enough for him. I thought he might have at least enjoyed himself a little. I felt like I'd failed him again. I blinked a couple of times; perhaps I could stop the tears prickling at the back of my eyes.

"This is a sentence. A two-week sentence and you're nothing but wardens. I hate you all." His voice wasn't accusatory. It was flat, delivered as resignation. His fists tensed. White knuckles nested on his thighs.

I exhaled. "Lucian, could I have done better?" I was still a novice at this; I'd tried to be as caring as possible. I wanted him to trust me. So as not to startle him, I gently held on to his wrists and pulled his fists away. He let me this time.

He huffed. "Don't care. It's my stupid head!" He jabbed at the side of his head and tore at a couple of the dark curls.

My heart felt the pain in those words. "You. Your head. You are not stupid."

"This." He waved his hands down the sides of his body. "This here is useless. I wish I could burst open and let everything out. Like you real people." His shoulders shook, but no tears came. He hiccupped from the earlier exertion and stared at the middle distance.

I feather-touched his shoulder with my right hand remembering how it all went wrong when I didn't respect his space. Today, he'd accepted my physical contact.

"You're not useless, Lucian."

He looked up, tears swam in his eyes but he didn't jerk away. A teardrop did fall down his cheek. "Then, why did my mum put me here? Why?" His voice shook, wavering with self-doubt.

"Your mum loves you. That's why she needs help from time to time." I was certain of that, just as I was sure of my own love and protectiveness towards Lucian. He'd have found it difficult to make the connection.

The teardrops froze on his long lashes.

He opened and shut his fists to try and relax. "My dad left because of me."

So, he heard.

Slowly, I shared my thoughts. "You know what? My dad left and it was nothing to do with me. He wanted to be with another woman." I let my tears fall, too. "I must have been hurt by his action, but now I'm glad that he's not with us. He didn't love us enough to stay, so he wouldn't have been any good if he did."

Lucian blinked.

Sam stepped up next to us. She knelt down to our level. "Lucian, I don't know your father, but sometimes people need an excuse to leave. Sometimes people are selfish. Your mum is not selfish for wanting you to be cared for by someone else for two weeks. She loves you. That much I know."

Lucian's body was finally under some degree of control. "She tells me she loves me, too." He turned in my direction. "I didn't hurt anyone this time. I tried to control myself."

I wiped my tears away and squeezed his hand gently. "Yes. That's good. You're doing great. I'm glad you can be home soon." I was proud of Lucian who'd participated as much as he could, who'd tried to overcome his disability with sheer will and determination.

I pointed to his colour pencils. "Why don't I help you arrange the colours?"

Lucian nodded and opened the case.

DAY 13

WE WERE COMPLETING another long trek. Only seven of the kids came along, including Eric and Lucian. Seven miles across relatively undulating terrain because of Eric's leg. Tim pretty much carried him the last couple of miles. It was hard graft, a test of our resolve.

We stopped for lunch by a reservoir. Lucian sat on a rock and stretched his legs out. He carefully peeled back the wrapped sandwich before eating it. I was really going to miss him.

I closed my eyes again, and all my senses were heightened: the sun on my button nose, the sounds of birds, the herby scents. When I re-opened my eyes, I saw Lucian glancing at me sidelong.

"You got it, Josie."

I smiled back even though he wasn't meeting my gaze. Even if I could never imagine what it felt like for Lucian, I loved the way he'd taught me how to tune in to my senses. "Yes, I do now. Thanks to you. Thank you for this lovely holiday."

He flapped his hand but said nothing for a while. "I don't hate you, Josie." He turned to face the other way.

I grinned. "I know you don't."

I became acutely aware that our time was running out.

***

Sam found me while I was communicating to my willow friend for the last time. The air was damp and grassy. The weather was changing as we prepared for our impending departure from the camp.

"I'm glad I took a detour." Sam's white teeth shone in the moonlight.

Sam had one of the two single rooms. Grant had the other. I wondered what her bedroom at home was like, and thought about my small box room that I'd soon be leaving behind. It had too many unnecessary girly possessions anyway. It was time to ditch them, and other emotions that might have come with being an ordinary, inexperienced young woman who hadn't seen enough of the world.

I sat on the edge of Sam's bed and rubbed her feet. A seven-mile walk wasn't normally a problem for her or for me, but having to help out some of the kids at the same time added a level of challenge. She grinned at me. Sam smelled of sun lotion—a mixture of coconut and lemon—a culinary impossibility but I'd forever associate summer with those scents.

Nights like this reminded me of a holiday in the Far East a long time ago, where my grandmother came from. It was a few years before my father left, so I was maybe six or seven. The air was always sultry and full of the synchronic sounds of the cicadas. They were like musicians in a symphony orchestra, all playing together and the tunes rose and fell as if coordinated. In the British summer time, we could hear the sizzling chaotic noises of bugs but no cicadas. I sometimes missed the East even though my memory of it was hazy, lying dormant only in my DNA. I told Sam about that and she smiled.

My eyes were drawn to a small discoloured mark on her leg. It was perhaps a faint birthmark. It stretched two inches from her knee. My fingers danced across it.

"It was a burn. My first holiday in Tehran, and on the first night I ran into the kitchen of my grandparents' house because they told me they'd bought me sweets. I tipped the pot of hot water on my leg." Sam considered her scar. "It served me right to expose my leg."

"You were young, weren't you?"

She covered my hand with her bigger one. "Yeah, I was too young to need covering up. I still haven't done that for any religious reasons."

I couldn't imagine her doing that either. A burn, a subversive act that had left a mark.

Even though we'd walked back from the stream without verbalising an arrangement, I was still unsure if she wanted me to be there. My head was lowered so I couldn't see her face and she wouldn't realise my warring emotions, between needing to know what it felt like and not wanting rejection. But, she didn't tell me it was impossible this time. We were returning home tomorrow. To our separate lives.

Lucian to his home. A cocoon that protected him.

Sam to her work in the city.

I realised I still knew next to nothing about her personal life. I'd avoided asking questions. *Do you have a girlfriend? Will I see you again?* I'd known the answers and didn't want them. When my rational brain took over and my heart lost the battle, it'd hurt. Though not then, not when the idea of being with each other was possible.

I'd move forward with my future. When I was eighteen, it had felt like forever. I had all the silly visions: we'd keep in touch, she'd come to visit me in London and we'd hold hands and walk down the city streets and through the royal parks; she'd wait for me to finish college. I knew damn well they were all futile dreams. Our days were numbered but precious.

Sam closed the distance and wound her strong arm around my shoulders, drawing me close. "Professional misconduct. I really shouldn't," she whispered, though I heard a lack of conviction in her own words.

Well, I was a volunteer. I didn't work for her as such, and I'd wanted her. *Informed consent.* Something that an eighteen-year-old should be able to give. Except I wasn't exactly informed or experienced. I found myself chuckling and all I could say was "Come on." She giggled in return.

The bed is so small. I found myself wondering what could happen in that narrow space.

Images of sex came into my mind, but they were always between men and women. I tried to think whether I'd seen anything that suggested otherwise. A young woman coy, waiting for the man to come and undress her. I decided that this was different. It had to be, and so I wasn't going to let Sam initiate it even if she seemed more experienced. For all I knew, she might have done this with a thousand girls before me. It didn't matter at that moment because when we touched each other's bare skin, all rational thoughts vanished.

A tear escaped the corner of my eye and Sam kissed it away. She kissed me all over, and her warm, strong hands were surprisingly soft and gentle on my body. I rubbed against her, and she pushed back. We were like creatures caught up in a tide, happy to be persuaded by the waves. We let the sensations take over, knowing full well it might be the only time we'd truly be free.

As if it was hard for her to admit doubt, she swallowed hard. "I probably shouldn't have done it."

I didn't want to hear the guilt in her voice, as if she'd violated me, which was untrue. I felt elated even though my performance seemed forced, as if I was merely playing a role. Hindsight was a powerful thing that twisted our perception. For a brief moment, fear flooded into my brain. Was I only one of many conquests? Sam was one of those women who wouldn't give a shit, and I was ripe for picking. I must have shaken my head. I wanted this. My mouth on her and hers on me kissing and arousing me once more.

I wanted to avoid the whole conversation about it being my first time. That reminder of my inexperience wouldn't do. It thrilled me to see Sam fall apart and come, her face inches away from mine, her eyes half-closed. The golden brown grew in depth.

I wondered how I appeared to her. I knew my face was flushed because of the heat and the sweat, making the air in the room muggy as a swamp.

Instead, I closed my eyes and smiled. "I want to get pregnant by you."

Sam laughed even though she tried to be quiet so no one would hear us. "That's the cutest thing I've heard in a long time." She kissed my cheek and brushed a strand of stray hair away from my forehead. "Anyway, you're too fucking young."

Yes, we were back to the age difference. Ten years. Later, when I'd had other partners, travelled, worked, I'd think back to that heady summer; twenty-eight would soon come to me, too. Then, I thought I loved her. I was in love. Innocent and passionate. I felt an intensity that I would never experience again.

I didn't recognise her vulnerability, because she was the leader, and leaders didn't falter. But she scratched her skull and sighed. "I hope it was okay. For you, I mean."

"Why wouldn't it be?"

"First time is important. I fear you've done it with the wrong person." Her voice was a whisper.

I closed my eyes against the light from her desk lamp. It was strong, bright beyond the dusk in the room. "I'm happy. I'm glad we did it, Sam," was my answer.

She stood, pulled on a vest and lit a cigarette out of the window. The smoke was pungent and swirly. I joined her, sticking my head out of the window into the chilled air of the night. She gazed at me intently, as if she was seeing a different person.

"Is it really Samantha? Your name, I mean." I'd been wanting to ask that question all week.

She chuckled. "It's Samira, actually. My mum's Iranian." I was reminded of her story about the family trip to Tehran.

"And I'm Jo to most people," I replied. I liked names like that. Short, androgynous. "My gran was half-Chinese. Can you tell? I don't have Asian facial features."

Sam smiled. "No, I couldn't tell, but you're beautiful."

I stared at the tattoo, half hidden under her short hair that had grown back a little over the past two weeks. I'd tried to remember how she looked. I couldn't bear the acid that was building as the night wore on; I was already suffering from the impending forced separation from her.

I couldn't stay all night. She walked me back to my room—the whole fifty yards that could well have been universes between us.

DAY 14

IN MY WILDEST fantasy, something grand—deus ex machina—would happen on the final day of the camp. But our routine seemed to continue like all previous mornings. We had breakfast. Lucian still couldn't quite stand the 'disgusting' orange juice, and he put his egg, toast and beans in exactly the same order. I helped him pack, even though everything was in neat piles already. He had a few extra stones and leaves that he'd collected, so I found a small box from the kitchen for him to put them in. The kids would leave first, mid-morning. He avoided my gaze. I wanted to tell him that he had wonderful clear blue eyes.

We stood outside the squat building. The pairs of hosts and guests said goodbye to each other. I wished I could have avoided this, while wanting to share one more moment with Lucian. He wrung his hands and shifted to the far end of the group, again.

"You'll miss me." It was a statement.

"Yes." Definitely. I'd always remember Lucian, the boy who showed me how to see with my mind's eye. "You're hard to forget, Lucian."

"And you'll remember the leader."

I didn't reply. He'd always known. Lucian was intuitive that way.

I took off my leather bracelet. I'd bought it during a music festival the year before. It had a small silver heart. I held it out. "For you. Would you like me to put it on?"

Lucian avoided looking at my face but he'd see the bracelet. "Okay." He stretched out his arm so I could put the thin strap on.

"Thank you." Lucian fingered the leather and was deep in thought for moments. He looked into his art bag and withdrew his drawing pad. He flipped through the pages and found one leaf. It was one of the beautiful sunflower drawings—the one I'd asked to keep. He pulled the sheet out carefully and handed it to me.

"For me?" My eyes widened. Tears threatened to surge.

He nodded.

I took his drawing. I wanted to tell him how much our time together meant to me. "Thank you. I'll cherish it. I'm glad to be here. Thank you for spending time with me." I probed, "You must be looking forward to going home."

Lucian blinked. "My mum needed a break. It's okay. I'm not upset now."

I stared at him and had the most urgent need to touch him. "May…may I hug you? I promise I won't crush you or anything."

He stiffened, then let his arms hang next to his sides. "Okay."

I went forward to him and encircled his tall, slender body. He tried to hug me back. His hands barely skated across my back, but it was enough.

When I let him go a few beats later, he smiled. "No meltdown."

"No meltdown." I grinned back.

"Goodbye, Josie." He picked up his holdall and turned to join the others in the waiting bus. I watched his strong back, his frame larger than his age suggested. He disappeared up the short flight of steps onto the bus.

I returned to my room and packed my bag, my mind blank. I'd been expecting this, but now a heavy load weighed on me. I took my large backpack and climbed the back of the van, refusing to search for her. Tim saved a seat for me again. I watched the landscape fly by. The sky had clouded over. The miraculous summer had come to an end.

The sky was threatening rain by the time we arrived back in the city. We stood where the van stopped, in the middle of an ugly car park on the back of Oxford Road, near the university.

Standing in the dreary concrete car park, it felt like death. Final and permanent. I didn't want us to end there. It was completely incongruent with whatever fleeting thing we had.

In my heart, I'd already begun to heal the hurt, to convince myself that this way was better, for whatever reason that only older adults would understand. It'd have been no use to explain it to my eighteen-year-old self. No use at all.

It wasn't easy to think about losing someone unless she had a name, a status. But Sam was beyond a label. And I understood too well she'd be gone forever, out of my life, after these goodbyes. I wished I could care less.

Sam kissed my cheek briefly. It was so light that a feather would seem like weight compared to it. She stood back, then, as if embarrassed. "You take care of yourself, okay?" she whispered. "Because I see your future. It's so radiant that I find it hard to watch. You keep going with that bright heart inside of you."

Tears stung the backs of my eyes. I wanted to say goodbye but the words wouldn't come, as though I knew whatever I said would seal our fate. We'd never see each other again, and by not bidding each other goodbye, we were preserving what we had. Nonetheless, sadness filled me. Deeply, overwhelmingly. I wished I could close my eyes and never see again if this was the last moment I laid my eyes on Sam.

I forced myself to open them. I was a grown-up, and grown-ups faced whatever life threw at them. I might as well start here.

Her girlfriend waited patiently in the car. Sam gazed over to her and back at me.

"Lucian means man of light. It's Latin," Sam uttered.

I managed to nod. I knew that. I also wanted us to kiss again, not a peck, but one that would have let me taste her again. Sam could see that in my face but she looked away.

"Why didn't you tell me?" I asked.

She bit her lip. "I wanted you, and you me. I think you did. Didn't you?"

Yes, I wouldn't have cared. I wouldn't have asked for a different outcome. I must have spoken aloud.

"I'm the one who's lost something. I'll miss out." She touched my arm. "I'm sorry."

"I'm not." I blinked back my tears. "And you don't get to tell me it's a silly holiday romance."

"Never." Her voice was so small but I heard it. I forced myself to grin, to show defiance.

She smiled, then, and ran over to the waiting vehicle, got in without looking back. I never asked for her number because I knew I wouldn't use it.

I tilted my head to see that the sun managed to shine through a gap in the rain clouds, and the glory hurt my eyes. I closed them and all I could see was the light imprinted in my mind. When I opened them again, their car had gone, and the tears crowded my eyes, shutting out the light. The white amidst Lucian's yellow. Since everyone from the camp had left, I let my tears fall. Yet I regretted nothing. I was crying from a grief for my childhood. But I was also happy in a way.

I'd found out that sometimes it only took fourteen days to change a life or two. I often wondered how three such disparate people should be brought together, serendipitously, randomly, and yet, our crossed lines exploded with lasting effects. It was as beautiful and exhilarating as fireworks.

My home town. It had started to drizzle. Instead of going home, I wandered around the area where Victorian warehouses had been turned into trendy shops and eateries, and apartments for young professionals. I stared at the pedestrians and felt angry. *How dare they go about their daily business as if nothing has happened.* I scanned their faces as I walked from the university through to the city's transport interchange. I knew I was close to the Gay Village. I'd been there numerous times with Jason, but I seemed to automatically dial up my gaydar. No, it was not about finding out that I was a lesbian. It was my first love. The first time

I'd given my heart to someone who couldn't reciprocate in the same way.

That became my modus operandi for many years, through college and afterwards. Sure, there were Sam-like girlfriends, wonderful companions in their own right, but no one could be the same as the first. No one could compare to her because she broke my fragile heart and brought so much wisdom to me. These women came close, but were never good enough. I'd learned to measure out my love, to rationalise, to hold back. I argued and broke up with them for no good reason. I wonder if Sam knew the effects she had on me.

I went back to volunteer for the camp the next year. *More accolade for my CV.* I recalled how I justified it. Tim was there, but I'd known in my heart that Sam and Lucian would be absent. Tim had smiled at me in the same open and kind way. *Sam's travelling the world. I've seen her photos from sunny climes. Lucky woman. She wanted to do it before she turned thirty.* Lucian and his mum had moved to Southampton where she came from. I wondered how Lucian would cope with such a big move. Not great, I assumed.

Eric could no longer come. *No, it's only for under-eighteens.* Oh, everyone grew old even though Lucian would always stay the same overgrown teenage boy in my memory. This reminded me that perhaps Lucian, too, was much taller and wiser. *Would he remember me?*

We talked for minutes about them. The camp kept us busy so there was no more time to dwell on our absent friends. One night, I sat with Tim by the campfire. Tears came suddenly. I pretended that my eyes were stung by the hot flame, but Tim guessed the real reason.

"Would you like her email?" He didn't need to name her.

I dried my face with the back of my hand. Sam was on the other side of the world, perhaps wondering what I was doing, whether I'd returned to the Peak District that summer. She might imagine my life as a young student in London, how I would date other people. Or, she might have completely forgotten about me. That would have killed me. I didn't want to write to her, pour my heart out for her not to bother replying. I couldn't bear it. Or if she replied and told me all about her adventures with another girl and pretended that our time didn't exist. No, that wouldn't do either.

"No, thank you."

"She's travelling alone." Tim cocked his head. "Are you sure?"

I understood what he was implying, but I wouldn't have changed my mind, and I didn't want to explain to Tim why not. It was better this way. Sam who took so much of me without realising. I couldn't explain to all my lovers why it was hard to love them with all my heart. I never told any of them about the true nature of that summer. Instead, I recited the way I'd come out. No, it wasn't a definitive moment. How had I known? It'd taken two weeks in the summer. Perhaps that wasn't the case. It was deeply seeded in me. Sam was only the water, and Lucian the light that helped me sprout.

For a while, I had photos of Sam on my mobile phone, but those images were grossly inadequate to represent my memory of what happened between us. Even years after I'd deleted those photos, I'd pick up a fork and remember Lucian and the way Sam's face was close to mine when she tended to the small stab wound. I'd smile and think of the teenager when I had pizza or spaghetti. In time, I'd lose the sharp edges of the visual images but something stayed with me.

A spark of light.

Pure as innocence.

~ The End ~

ABOUT SEASONS OF LOVE

Love follows no rules. Like sun in winter and rain in summer, love can blossom in the most unexpected places. This richly diverse collection of stories proves that love is as universal and as varied as the seasons.

The Stories:

- *Tourist Season* – Deven Balsam
- *Machete Betty and the Office Sharks* – Neptune Flowers
- *Once Around Seven* – Ofelia Gränd
- *Winter Blossoms* – Paul Iasevoli
- *Year of the Guilty Soul* – A.M. Leibowitz
- *The Great Village Bun Fight* – Debbie McGowan
- *A Springful of Winters* – Dawn Sister
- *Out of Season* – Bob Stone
- *Seashell Voices* – Alexis Woods
- *Courting Light* – A. Zukowski

Available as a complete anthology (ebook/paperback)
and as individual stories (ebook + longer stories in paperback).

For more information/purchase links, visit:
www.beatentrackpublishing.com/SeasonsofLove

ABOUT A. ZUKOWSKI

I am a London-based British writer who grew up in the gay village and red light district of Manchester, UK.

I was trained in screenwriting at the University of the Arts, London; National Film & Television School and Script Factory, UK, followed by a series of misadventures as a film journalist, writer and producer of short films. My stories are based on personal and emotional experiences, and feature strong LGBTQ-identified characters.

Connect with the Author

Blog: http://azukowskiblog.wordpress.com

Goodreads: http://www.goodreads.com/author/show/16509569.A_Zukowski

FB: http://www.facebook.com/aleksander.zukowski.353

Smashwords: http://www.smashwords.com/profile/view/azukowski

Twitter: http://twitter.com/saszazukowski

Tumblr: http://azukowski.tumblr.com

BY A. ZUKOWSKI

The Boy Who Fell to Earth (#1 London Stories)

Liam For Hire (#2 London Stories)

BEATEN TRACK PUBLISHING

For more titles from Beaten Track Publishing,
please visit our website:

http://www.beatentrackpublishing.com

Thanks for reading!

www.ingramcontent.com/pod-product-compliance
Lightning Source LLC
Chambersburg PA
CBHW020624130626
46552CB00003B/1090